TYPECASTING FOR A KILLER

CAROLINE AMBROSE
the violet-eyed leading lady—how far would she go to keep an ingenue off center stage ... and away from her leading man?

EDDIE LAFFERTY
a method actor playing a madman—what makes him so right for the role?

GEORGINA PHILLIPS
the platinum blonde Bride of Dracula—what is the secret that can get her thrown out of the play?

KAREN SNOW
the chic but sweet stage manager—who is she trying to protect?

ARTHUR DARIEN
the desperate director—why did he hire a private eye to cover a case when he's not willing to tell the whole truth?

Now detective Michael Spraggue joins this sinister theatre company and looks for the clues to the character who keeps murder as an understudy.

BLOOD WILL HAVE BLOOD

Linda Barnes

FAWCETT CREST • NEW YORK

In memory of Peter

Acknowledgment

I'd like to thank James Morrow, Jacki
Forbes, and Richard Barnes for their
comments, criticism, and encouragement.

A Fawcett Crest Book
Published by Ballantine Books
Copyright © 1982 by Linda Appelblatt Barnes

Library of Congress Catalog Card Number: 81-52406

ISBN 0-449-20901-6

         tured in the United States of America

         ne Books Edition: March 1986

Chapter One

"So what's the big deal?" Spraggue said. "Nobody's ever quit on you before?"

"Not one week before goddam opening night!" Arthur Darien shook his balding head vigorously. "It must have been the Bloody Marys. That really got to him."

Spraggue nodded, said nothing. Darien had requested—*demanded*—the conference. As soon as he tired of his own ranting, the story would spill over.

"Listen, Michael," Darien said abruptly, "the Bloody Marys, all the damned pranks, have some connection to the Dracula legend—like the garlic the bastard put in Mina's sewing basket."

"Chases away the vampires," said Spraggue.

"Right." Darien beamed approvingly. "And when you kill a vampire you have to cut off his head and stuff it with garlic."

"Pleasant task."

"Prevents him from rising."

"The severed head alone might do that," said Spraggue.

"So goes the legend."

"Right. Who got the snootful of garlic, Arthur? Who plays Mina?"

"Caroline Ambrose. Remember her? Tony Award. Great actress. But then, I've got a terrific cast, an all-around dynamite company—"

"Arthur," Spraggue interrupted. He couldn't blame Darien for moving past the subject of Ambrose as quickly as possible. Caroline Ambrose: almost enough right there to make an actor quit a paying job. "You know, garlic in sewing baskets doesn't seem very apocalyptic to me."

"Michael, that's the tip of the iceberg. Lights flicker onstage.

5

Someone hums this haunting, eerie tune, enough to make your blood freeze. Actors see strange figures in the darkness. . . ."

As Darien spoke, he stared. Spraggue sat motionless, relaxed under the scrutiny. At least the Royal Academy of Dramatic Art taught that much. Spraggue controlled a smile. Had he stood up under Darien's famous glare as well at their first meeting? He doubted it. He'd been—what?—nine, ten years younger. Just twenty-one, a Harvard dropout, a mere apprentice in a British repertory company come up to London to audition for the great American director, Arthur Darien.

"Why don't you tell me exactly why Frank quit?" said Spraggue.

Darien took a deep breath, bulging out his pink baby cheeks. He searched for a way to avoid answering the question, gave it up, shrugged, and began. "Frank Hodges had a passion for vodka. He'd make a pitcher of drinks at home, fill a thermos, and leave it in his dressing room. During breaks he'd visit his cache. He never really overdid it. I won't work with an alcoholic. . . ." Darien's voice threatened to trail off, then regained strength. "He handled it, like I said. Then two days ago, he nips downstairs, pours himself a quick one, and gulps it down—" Darien paused dramatically.

He can't help it, thought Spraggue. He's been around actors so long. He stole Darien's punch line with a grin. "And somebody'd switched Frank's Bloody Marys with the weekly Red Cross donation."

"You didn't have to speak to the guy! You didn't have to *look* at him. He'd thrown up. There were still flecks at the corners of his mouth—"

"I get the idea."

"Frank quit. He wouldn't even talk it over. Said there was a lunatic in the company. I couldn't keep him."

"Arthur," Spraggue said, "are you offering me a part in your play?"

Darien relaxed into a smile. "I always said you were an abrupt bastard. I'm giving you background, Michael. This is a tough business to explain and it's going to take me a little while."

"Then it's not a part," Spraggue said flatly. Time for the old financial touch.

"Dammit! Sit down! Yes, it's a part, but there's something else, something more."

"Money?"

"No."

Spraggue sat. Darien fumbled with a pipe, lit it.

"Smoke doesn't bother you, does it?" he asked.

"I'll open the window." Spraggue was glad of the chance.

"Nothing but exhaust fumes out there."

Window open, pipe lit, Darien focused his eyes on a space over Spraggue's head and resumed speaking. "Remember that trouble we had in London?" he said. "That girl—"

That incredible woman. Spraggue was no longer sitting in a cramped office, breathing stale smoke. He was riding on top of a red double-decker bus, laughing at the rain while—

"You helped the company out then." Darien's voice brought him back. "It was hushed up, but I found out."

"It was nothing. Petty thievery."

"The situation could have gotten out of hand. Tempers were frayed—"

"Did you invite me here to reminisce, Arthur? After all these years?"

"You're not making this any easier, Michael. I know you were a private investigator for a while—"

"I don't do it anymore. It didn't work out.".

Arthur Darien folded his plump hands on his desk. "With Frank gone, I do have a cast opening: Dr. John Seward. Not a lead, but not a support, either. An odd role, a young character part. Seward's an alienist. Brainy. Runs an asylum. One of his patients is in Dracula's power."

"Renfield," said Spraggue.

"You *do* remember the book."

"The movie. Bela Lugosi was one of my heroes."

"Read the book. It's an amazing work. Dark and hypnotic, frightening and real. Stoker tapped some source of primal horror, some phenomenon I doubt even he understood. You'll feel the power." Darien inhaled, coughed pipe smoke. "The play it could be, *should* be, hasn't hit the stage yet. That old Deane-Balderston melodrama barely caught the flavor of the book. There was so much those guys couldn't say, couldn't even hint at in the twenties. Hell, back then, the word stomach wasn't mentioned in polite society! Sex scenes were taboo! And, God, the technical advances alone! New fog machines! Projected scenery! Deane and Balderston had to set their show totally in England. We can go from Transylvania to England and back to Transylvania again, really follow the three-part structure of the

7

novel! And, *I've got a cast,* an incredible cast! For Dracula: John Langford. Is that inspired?"

Spraggue whistled under his breath. Langford. He'd make up for Ambrose and then some.

"And there's romance," Darien said teasingly. "Seward's in love with Dracula's first English victim, Lucy. Emma Healey plays Lucy."

At least he wouldn't have to make love to Caroline Ambrose. "The name's not familiar, Arthur. Should it be?"

"No, but the body should. Glorious redhead. Advertises suntan muck on the tube. You've seen her. Deep tan, tiny white bikini. A credit to lewdness in advertising. Your love scenes should be spectacular."

"Strictly Victorian, I'll bet."

"If I were your age, *I'd* grab the part. Even if I didn't get to ball Emma on stage! There's always an occasional afternoon off! And Seward's a fascinating guy. Introspective, but not passive. More Horatio than Hamlet. Very active at the climax of the play."

"And what's your other offer—"

"And you could play him, Michael." Darien rode over the interruption. "You're an *actor.* The years away from the profession don't matter. You're back now. God, I envy you that face, that adaptability. Your nose is a nose, your mouth is a mouth. Nothing outstanding but those cat's eyes. You've got that wonderful variety. You remind me of Laurence Olivier when he was young."

Spraggue lifted one eyebrow. The very best butter, he thought. The hidden half of the deal must be pretty raw.

He waited. It was hard to rush Arthur Darien. He studied the room, made an actor's exercise of memorizing the contents.

Darien's office in the old Fens Theater was small and musty, stuffed with old theatrical props. The little director was dwarfed by the mahogany throne he sat in. A bishop's chair, probably salvaged from some long-forgotten run of *Murder in the Cathedral.* At least it looked comfortable. Spraggue's own rickety chair must have seen service in a French drawing-room farce. Fake plants almost blocked the single window: the conservatory scene from *The Importance of Being Earnest.* The room had more doors than windows, two heavy wooden ones besides the entry from the hallway. A huge boarded-up fireplace filled the far wall. Over it: crossed swords. *Cyrano de Bergerac.* The daggers beneath were Macbeth's. Or would Macbeth have

8

used knives with that curious cross motif etched into the brass handles?

No decanters decorated the top of the sideboard. No bottles on the windowsill. No smell of whiskey. Darien's hands were nervous, but steady. Very different from the last time they'd met.

"We're doing vital work here, Michael," Darien said finally.

Spraggue nodded dutifully. Off on another tangent.

"All New York wants is gimmicks, musicals, glitter, and flash! Here, away from that madness, we can rebuild. This theater was due for the wreckers when I found it. Can you believe that? An exquisite relic like this? And historic! The last legit playhouse built in Boston. Home of the glorious Boston Rep, the best damn resident stock company in America. Their director poured his entire family fortune into this theater. No scrimping. The very finest equipment: turntables, fly space, wonderful lighting positions—"

"Did he make his money back?"

"You kidding?" Darien laughed, a full rich roar, and the London days came flooding back. "Theater's always been a lousy investment. The talkies came in, theater bombed. The old guy went broke. Samuel Borgmann Phelps, his name was. Ever heard of him?"

"No."

"The last of his kind. A true nineteenth-century man of the theater. He did *everything*—directed, produced, even built his own playhouse. A man of vision, a man of dreams—"

"What happened when the money ran out?"

"A man with a great sense of theater. When his last show folded, he opened the grand drape, trained the spots on center stage, and hung himself from the catwalk. An unforgettable closing night. A few of my cast members figure he still haunts the place."

"Do they think he fed Frank his bloody Bloody Marys?"

Darien concentrated on an ant crossing his desk. "I didn't tell the cast about Frank. I was afraid to stir up trouble. I told them something—some personal reason he had to leave. I couldn't risk losing anyone else so close to opening. The actors are nervous as hell."

Here it comes, thought Spraggue.

"Michael, I need your help. You could stop this joker. You'd be there, in the company, onstage—"

"Spying," Spraggue added flatly.

"This play deserves a chance to be born." Darien's voice dropped. "I want a chance. Everything I own is tied up in this project. I *need* this play! I can't just let it go!"

Spraggue shifted in the uncomfortable chair. He could feel the iron seat beneath its tiny pink cushion. "May I suggest you call in the police?"

"I want a show, not an investigation! Imagine rehearsals with the troops belching in the balcony! Picture the publicity! Absolutely not."

"Arthur." Spraggue waited until Darien's wide blue eyes met his before he spoke. "Is there anyone you suspect? If there is, tell me now."

"If I knew, if I had any idea, I'd tackle the bastard myself."

"Is there anyone you can positively eliminate?"

"Yes." Darien closed his eyes, rubbed his temples with shaky fingertips. "First of all, the crew. The disturbances started before they came up from New York. My house manager, Dennis Boland. He was out of town when a few of the pranks were pulled. My stage manager—no. You'll have to leave her in."

"Her?"

"Karen Snow. Excellent stage manager. Very professional."

"That leaves the cast, Arthur."

Darien threw up his hands. The feeling, Spraggue supposed, was sincere. The gesture was pure theater. "I can't believe any one of my actors would try to hurt this show. Why, Michael? Why would anyone want to—"

"That's the question," Spraggue agreed. "Why?"

Darien shoved a dark blue folder across the desk top. "Then you'll do it? I knew—well, let's say I hoped you would. Here's the script. Nine o'clock tomorrow morning. . . ."

"Wait a minute. No commitment yet. If you're really serious about this, I'll need a lot more than a lousy script. I'll need a cast list, a crew list, résumés, a list of your financial backers—"

Darien held up a silencing hand. "I have responsibilities toward those people. I can't give you any money stuff. Look"—he was thinking hard—"how's this? You can meet the backers next week. I'm going to throw a party, a gala like the ones old Phelps used to host when the theater first opened. The backers will all be there and—"

"I'm supposed to sit on my butt for a week? There's not enough time as it is. Too many people involved, too many possibilities."

Darien waved the script in front of Spraggue's eyes. "Just read

10

it," he pleaded. "Come back tomorrow and give me your answer."

"I can give you half an answer now. I'd like to play Seward. But one week—"

"Hell, Spraggue, you're a quick study. If I didn't know you could do it, I wouldn't have spent three days tracking you down. I had to call your aunt personally, beg her to get you to come and talk to me. I'm not saying it'll be easy." He jerked open the top desk drawer, located a single sheet of paper. "Here's a rehearsal schedule. We're well into the crunch; you won't get a day off for two weeks—"

Spraggue lifted his eyes from the neatly printed timetable. "And then it'll be Monday."

"Right. It's good-bye weekends."

"Matinees on Sundays," Spraggue said.

"And Wednesdays," Darien added. "I know you don't need the money, Spraggue—"

"But I'd like the work."

"I was hoping you'd say that."

"It's just that the other half of the deal doesn't exactly smell like lilacs to me."

"You'd be helping all of us. The actors are *scared*. Hell, I'm scared."

Spraggue got to his feet. "I'll read the script," he said.

"That's all I can ask."

The hallway felt miraculously cool and dark after the overheated office. Spraggue shut the door and stood silently for a minute, reviewing the conversation in his mind. Arthur Darien . . . It wasn't his words; they were mundane enough. It was just that you never got a chance to realize how ordinary they were while Darien spoke. He fixed you with that blue-eyed stare, turned the full force of his personality on you, and you succumbed. What an actor he would have made! What an actor he was.

Spraggue heard the door click and moved hastily forward. He didn't want the director to collide with his backside. But the door stayed shut; Darien didn't emerge. One of the other doors to the office must have opened. Inside, voices murmured. Spraggue moved off down the hall, but not before one sentence caught his ear.

"I just hope you know what you're doing," said an oily voice that was not Arthur Darien's.

11

Chapter Two

Spraggue waited for the Dudley bus at the corner of Mass Ave and Huntington. The hazy late-August heat was little improvement over Darien's stuffy office. Not even a breeze to rattle the piles of broken beer bottles and empty Coke cans.

A chance to act for Arthur Darien again. A good role in a successful play. All Darien's shows worked—when he was sober.

Why were there always goddam strings attached?

Usually the pitch was financial. A part, yes, but would Spraggue be willing to guarantee just a bit of the backing? No? So sorry, but the part was taken . . . A *name* actor, a *star* would be needed. At least Darien wasn't after cash.

The bus came, backfiring flatulently. Spraggue boarded along with a floral-hatted matinee contingent from Symphony. He stood at the back of the bus—less crowded there.

A spy, a company spy. In the cast, but not *of* it. An outside observer, reporting every innocent conversation, each misunderstood gesture, straight to Arthur Darien.

He got off at Harvard Square, end of the line, and walked the mile home.

The box was centered exactly in front of the door of the Fayerweather Street triple-decker. It was wrapped in creased brown paper that had started life as a shopping bag, and tied with limp white string. His name was penciled in block capitals: MICHAEL VINCENT SPRAGGUE III. No address; it hadn't come through the mail.

His name was spelled right. So many people, tricked by the long A, gave the last name only one G. Of course, when they realized the family connection, knew he was one of *the* Spraggues, the mistake never occurred. Great-grandfather

Davison Spraggue had taken care of that. Gossip columnists, hustlers, senators with bottomless campaign chests, they all knew how to spell Spraggue.

The sidewalk was clear. Two kids rolled a red dump truck up a tree root across the street. They didn't look up; too busy rerouting pebbles.

Spraggue hefted the box and climbed the stairs to the second floor.

The package was light—box, string, wrapping, and all came to not more than two pounds. Fourteen inches wide, a foot long, maybe three inches deep. It made a slight rustling noise when he shook it. He set the box on the kitchen table.

If he were still a licensed private eye, he'd be more suspicious, Spraggue decided. Fingerprint the paper? Useless. Too rough. Maybe open the whole shebang under water in the kitchen sink.

With his pocket knife, he cut the string.

There was birthday wrapping under the brown paper. Mickey and Minnie Mouse cavorted with Donald Duck. Huey, Dewey, and Louie danced in a circle around a pink-iced cake decorated with three flaming candles.

The box was plain white cardboard. No department-store name. No card. The sides of the lid were taped to the bottom. Spraggue slit the tape neatly with the knife.

Tissue paper. Spraggue patted the thin white film, spread it back.

At least the bat was dead. No doubt about that. Gray-brown wings opened wide, held with pins to a cardboard backing. The thin membrane of the right wing was ripped almost in two. Maybe when he'd shaken the box. . . .

The furry body, amazingly mouselike, was small and shriveled. The head, completely severed from the body, was pinned an inch above the dark stain that marked where it should have been. Another pin stuck out of the tiny gaping mouth.

Spraggue swallowed twice, pushed the mess away, reached for the phone. Darien answered on the third ring.

"Arthur," Spraggue said, "who knows about me?"

"What?"

"Did you tell the cast you were planning to offer me Seward? The crew? Anyone?"

"No." Darien's response was definite.

"When you called my aunt, did you do it from your office?" That would be as private as skywriting over the Charles River. Three doors. Eavesdropper heaven.

"I may have. I think I did. Why?"

"Thanks, Arthur."

"Don't hang up! Why did you want to know about—"

"Nothing, Arthur. Never mind."

"Michael?" Darien's tone was hopeful. "Have you thought it over? I don't mean to put the pressure on—"

"I haven't even started reading the damn script." The words died on Spraggue's tongue. He glanced at the beheaded bat, resting in fragments of bright wrapping paper.

"I'll take the part," he said.

Chapter Three

"Places!"

"Get with it! Cut the work lights!"

"Just *minimal* blues between scenes! Take 'em down another point. Set it! Start with 47B. Preset 10. Okay?"

"Can I take the house lights out?" The stage manager shaded her eyes, stared expectantly at the center section of the orchestra. Experience rather than sight told her where Arthur Darien sat. The director nodded, then realized that the spotlights effectively blinded the woman.

"Please, Karen," he shouted back.

Karen Snow, stage manager. Spraggue checked her off on his mental shopping list. Didn't look as tough as she sounded. Her voice was too big for her body. She gave a curt nod of her sleek dark head and paced steadily off into the wings. Authority set her tiny figure apart. In all the chaos of the long morning, Spraggue realized, he had never seen the stage manager run, never heard her voice go shrill.

A fat man glided across the carpeted auditorium and sat delicately in the seat next to Arthur Darien's. His face was as round and smooth as his body; his hair dark and greasy for one so pale. He folded his hands neatly over his belly, hiding the gap where his vast blue shirt failed to meet his navy pants.

Darien smiled, said hello. He called the fat man Dennis. Dennis. That would be the house manager, Dennis Boland. One more for the shopping list. Out of the running, Darien had said. Out of town when—

"Curtain!" The lights dimmed then came up slowly, deep blue shrouded in mist. The faint beams lit the unfinished set to advantage. All the scenery was constructed on a revolving platform. One semicircle handled the Westenra house and

17

various rooms in Dr. Seward's sanatorium. The other side in stark contrast to the realistic Victorian interiors, consisted entirely of steps, landings, and platforms—a constructivist approach to both the rocky seaside at Whitby and the ancient battlements of Castle Dracula.

Now the setting was Transylvania, a chamber in the vampire's ancestral home.

The two actresses on stage, Spraggue decided, looked even better together than they did separately. Side by side, blond Georgina Phillips's slight figure emphasized brunette Deirdre Marten's model height. The blonde looked platinum; the brunette's silky hair glistened jet black. Together, the brides of Dracula were a testament to the excellent taste of the Vampire King.

Georgina muffed a line, broke character, groped for the correct words.

"Stop!" Arthur Darien's voice, world-weary, cut in. Spraggue grinned. God, he remembered that tone, that disappointed you've-failed-me-again sigh, that dreadful forebearance. Ten years ago, Michael Spraggue, the novice actor, had found it soul-shattering. Even now, he was glad not to be its target.

"Take ten," the voice continued sadly.

Footsteps. Darien and the playwright left the auditorium. The dark-haired woman floated wordlessly off into the wings. The blonde bride, a pink flush settling over her round face, made a beeline for Spraggue's first-row seat.

"Another rewrite break!" she announced with a moan. "It'll be *my* lines that go. Every time I open my mouth on that stage I can just *feel* Darien suffer. Did you notice?"

"No," said Spraggue truthfully. "Maybe it's just a technical thing."

She flashed him a quick smile. "Honestly, I don't know why he ever cast me!"

A tall straw-blond man executed an elegant pirouette in the aisle, leaned languidly against a chair. "A man with Darien's reputation for the ladies, *especially* the younger ladies, and you can't *imagine* why he cast you? Isn't that sweet!" He had a tenor that threatened to lisp.

"Shut up, Greg," said Georgina. "You're just jealous."

"Ooooooh," said Greg. "Is that supposed to mean that you think *I* harbor disgusting perverted desires for the old man?"

Georgina giggled. "Relax, Greg. Darien's got the hots for nothing but his show." She sighed deeply. "Don't I know it?"

She turned back to Spraggue apologetically. "You haven't met Greg yet, have you? Greg, this is Michael Spraggue, our new Seward."

"Delighted!" Greg leaned gracefully over and shook Spraggue's hand with a light, cool grip. "How lovely to have *actors* to work with a week before opening! Not that the stage manager hasn't done a bang-up job reading your lines, but she is *female*—and definitely not an *actress*. So hard to establish *rapport* with a nonentity. Gregory Hudson is the full name. I play Jonathan Harker, stalwart husband to Mina, our leading lady."

"Caroline Ambrose," Georgina filled in helpfully.

Greg laughed, a high tenor squeal. "She makes me feel so *inadequate*—so inexperienced. After all, she's had *five* husbands in real life, while *I*—"

"Still bad-mouthing my fellow star?" Spraggue hadn't seen the redheaded woman approach. Now that she stood next to him, he wished she'd go back up to the top of the aisle and start again. She deserved to be watched. Alone or in a Miss America pageant, here was a knockout. Spraggue decided on a career as a connoisseur of suntan-oil commercials.

The redhead smiled and touched his hand. "I'm Emma Healey," she said. "Arthur told me where to find you, Michael. But I think I would have recognized you even if he hadn't warned me. From your film, the British one—"

"I thought no one saw that." Spraggue answered her smile.

"I did. Very good."

"Thanks. It was a long time ago."

Emma's voice was terrific, low and warm. She turned away but Greg held her, a possessive arm firmly around her waist. Spraggue stared. Maybe he had summed up the lanky pretty-boy too quickly.

"What was that you said about *fellow* star, Emma dear?" Greg said. "Caroline Ambrose, *your* equal? Come off it, darling. Who has the private dressing room? The coach? The suite at the Ritz-Carlton? The orchids delivered daily?"

"Those have nothing to do with the show," protested Emma.

"But they have a lot to do with the Caroline Ambrose mystique."

Georgina dropped into the seat next to Spraggue. "Do you really think she sends them to herself?" she asked slyly.

Spraggue shrugged. "I thought they emanated from some former husband or other."

"Divorced or the one they say she killed?"

"If he's dead, Georgie, I doubt they'd even let him in the flower shop." Greg leaned over and patted Georgina on the head.

Emma laughed. "Oh, Georgina, have you been reading the fan mags again?"

Georgina blushed. "Well, they *do* say terrible things about her. And she *has* been married five times. How old is she, anyway?"

"Old enough to play Dracula," said Greg.

"Then how did she get the part?"

Greg winked at Spragge. "Listen to our ingénue prattle!" He spoke to Georgina as if she were a slow two-year-old. "*Old friends*, darling. She and Darien are *old friends. Close* friends, too."

"I know the story of the orchids," Emma said quietly.

"Tell all, darling, instantly!"

Emma peered cautiously left and right. The stagehands rushed about, shepherded by the stage manager. No other actors were within earshot. Ambrose was on call, but probably still lazed in her dressing room. She preferred isolation and special treatment to the instant camaraderie of her colleagues.

With a wicked gleam in her eye, Emma stepped to the center of the aisle and performed her story à la Shirley Temple.

"Once upon a time," she lisped, "Princess Caroline was married to a gorgeous South American millionaire. This was after her first two marriages, you understand, and before her last two. He was tall and dark and very handsome, although he was much older than our Caroline. He owned all the coffee beans and all the pineapples and all the orchids in Colombia."

Emma struck a tragic pose, one hand flattened against her brow, and continued. "They met when he visited New York and adored Caroline in *Strange Interlude*. He went backstage. Our Caroline, bored with her second husband and sniffing endless cash, bedazzled him."

"I don't know how she does it," said Georgina. "I haven't even been married once!"

Emma turned. "Don't interrupt! He whisked Princess Caroline off to his homeland and, somewhat belatedly, wed her. Rumors began to issue from the jungle. She was pregnant. She wasn't pregnant. She'd lost a child, perhaps deliberately. Her husband beat her. She beat him. You know the stuff. After a year, Caroline reappeared in New York, alone. She filed for divorce on grounds of extreme mental cruelty." Emma's voice

20

rose to a crescendo. "And now, every day, she gets a memento of that happy year: orchids from the Colombian's equatorial plantation. If she's acting, they arrive at the theater; between shows, at her domicile—"

"Sort of like DiMaggio and the red roses on Marilyn's grave," sighed Georgina.

Greg snorted. "At least *he* had the decency to wait until she was dead!"

Georgina ignored him. "You'd think he'd have given it up after she remarried. . . ."

"Caroline got two dozen white orchids the day she married Harvey What's-his-name," Emma said. "That little affair only lasted six months or so and the flowers kept on arriving. Caroline didn't protest. There's a certain amount of notoriety, press coverage, et cetera, in being the Orchid Lady."

"Maybe," said Georgina dreamily, "he does it to make her feel guilty for leaving him. You know, one day the orchids won't arrive and she'll wonder why and then she'll pick up a newspaper and read his obituary and—"

Greg giggled. "Georgie, you're wasted here. Really. Why don't you write for the soaps?"

"Well, it *is* a good story." Georgina looked questioningly at Emma. "*If* it's true."

Emma smiled down at the earnest blonde. "As far as I know, honey, it's true."

"We'll just have to get Lady Caroline to come up and play Truth with the peons one of these days," said Greg.

"Truth?" asked Georgina.

"It's a game, darling. A lovely game."

"What are you up to now, Greg?" Emma's eyes narrowed. They were an incredibly intense emerald. Spragge couldn't remember ever seeing eyes that exact shade. They made him wonder about contact lenses.

"I just thought we might have a game of Truth to pass the time," said Greg with a great show of injured innocence.

"Darien only called a ten-minute break—" began Spragge.

"Rewrite breaks take *forever*," Greg interrupted.

"Darien might remember," Georgina said hopefully. "He might realize we're all waiting and send someone to give us the okay. Then we could go out for a drink or—"

"Darien? Remember the peasants?" Greg gave his curious squealing laugh. "*If*, by chance, he should notice the time, he will send a messenger straight down to the dressing rooms where that *great* British actor, John Langford, holds court with Caroline, Our Lady of the Flowers—"

"Gus Grayling's down there, too," said Georgina. "Have you met him, Michael?"

"No."

"If Grayling *is* down there," continued Greg, "it is only on sufferance. He'd certainly be a third wheel, what with Caroline bent on making Langford husband No. 6. Remember, as Van Helsing, Gus may have the most lines in the play, but Count Dracula is the *lead*. And"—Greg turned to Emma—"*if* we were to tempt Lady Caroline to play Truth with us, she would certainly tell you that she is the *star*."

"I'll play," said Georgina. "If you'll teach me."

Greg winked at Emma. "We'll need more victims, don't you think?"

"Let's see. Me and you and Georgie and Michael." She grinned at Spraggue and he decided he might not mind being a victim. "We'll get Eddie! He'd love to play."

"With you, dear Emma, I doubt it. With our lovely stage manager, now. . . ."

"Have you seen him, Greg?" Emma cut the blond man off.

"Really burns you, doesn't it, darling? So young, so insensible to your overwhelming charms. . . . Good for him. Some men ought to be able to resist you. Right, Spraggue?"

Spraggue looked at Greg curiously. His tone said clearly: keep away from Emma. Spraggue shrugged. It was a little difficult to keep his eyes off the tight, low-cut blue leotard Emma had chosen as rehearsal wear. It gave rise to some speculation. She hardly bounced, but her nipples were clearly outlined against the tight-stretched cloth. Excellent musculature or a very thin bra. Her jeans boasted a designer's name scrawled across the molded ass.

"Eddie!" Emma called toward backstage. "Come on! We're playing a game and you're it!"

As soon as Eddie lumbered on stage, Spraggue knew he must play the madman, Renfield. Mostly, it was the eyes. Large, wide, far-apart eyes. If they'd been brown, they'd have been fine— warm, dark, puppy-dog eyes. But they were cold, staring blue, slightly watery. Discomforting eyes. A pair of hornrimmed glasses stuck out of his breast pocket.

"Is it that sensitivity shit?" he asked good-naturedly, vaulting down from the stage to join the group in the front row. "My

22

acting teacher doesn't hold with that junk. Said I should learn to speak."

"Ah, yes, enunciation!" Emma sucked in her breath and stood up tall, an inspiring sight.

"The arts and English literature!" echoed Georgina.

"Shakespeare!" Greg trumpeted. He bowed his head. "When will we see his like again?"

"Shut up," said Eddie calmly. "What's going on?"

"Truth!" answered Greg in a whisper.

Georgina raised a hand prettily. "Doesn't this game have any rules?"

"Of course! Eyes on a level," commanded Emma. "Everyone sit on the floor, cross-legged."

"Unless modesty forbids," Georgina said. She was wearing a skirt.

"Emma has no modesty," said Greg. "The first truth!"

"How do you play?" asked Georgina.

"It's like this," Greg began. "We go around the circle. Everyone has to tell one truth—"

"Something you've never told anyone before!" added Emma.

"Does it have to be about yourself?" asked Georgina uncertainly.

"Unless you've got the dirt on someone else here!"

"Who starts?"

"Emma!" Greg said positively. "She has the most lurid past, tells the most fascinating tales, and takes forever. Then we run out of time and no one else has to give."

Emma shook her head. "Let's start with someone new," she said coyly. "Fresh blood. How about it, Michael?"

"No!" said Georgina. She blushed and looked around the circle. "It's not fair. I mean, this is his first day and—"

Sprague smiled at the little blonde gratefully. He had a few truths he'd just as soon keep to himself.

Greg laughed. "Then *you,* Georgie. You'll have to take Michael's place."

"Come on," Emma said softly. "Just tell us one teeny truth and we'll let you alone."

Georgina breathed deeply and looked at no one. "Since everybody seems to know," she said finally, "I'll make it official. I have a crush on Arthur Darien. I like older men."

Emma raised a perfect eyebrow. "Why not Grayling then? He's older than hell—and he's always panting after you!"

23

"Is *that* why you've got the picture of that old coot in your dressing room?" asked Greg simultaneously. "Boyfriend, Georgie?"

"My grandfather!" The blush spread over Georgina's cheeks and down her throat. "And while we're on truths, I wish you'd all call me Gina, not Georgie. Gina's my professional name."

"That's just it," answered Greg. "Gina *sounds* like a professional name. Some women are Ginas; some are Georgies. To me, you're a Georgie."

"You're next, Greg," said Emma. Georgina shot her a relieved smile.

"Let's go the other way 'round the circle," said Greg.

"Let's not," said Spraggue.

"Come on!"

"Okay, okay! How's this one? Short and sweet." Greg held up both hands for silence. "When I was twelve years old I slept with my first cousin."

"And was your cousin a him or a her?" asked Emma sweetly.

"Now, now, darling. No explanations. A simple truth, that's all. And I assure you, it *is* the truth and I've *never* told anyone before." He nodded at Eddie, next in the circle. "Over to you."

Eddie's wide blue eyes focused on a spot in the group's center. "Arthur Darien's drinking again," he said quietly. "The pressure must be getting to him."

The circle was silent. Then everyone spoke at once.

"How do you know?"

"Bullshit!"

"Have you seen him?"

"That's not truth, that's opinion."

"Next!"

"Don't you even want to talk about it?" Eddie asked. "One week before opening? A new Dr. Seward. All those strange little happenings. . . ."

"Shut up!" They were all startled by the venom in Emma's tone. "It's my turn and I've got a truth for all of you. This is the first show I've ever had a lead in that I felt was going someplace! I want it to work! *And I am not the company ghost.* I think it's a good truth and I'd like you all to repeat it. We'll just go right around the circle and see if everybody else can say the same."

"Wait a minute," wailed Greg. "Emma, this is just a *game.* I didn't mean it to get so serious. . . ."

"I'm willing to play," Georgina said calmly.

"Anybody want out?" Emma asked.

Complete silence.

"Places!" came a strong female voice from onstage. "Let's go! Places: Act One, scene three!"

Chapter Four

For a frozen second, no one moved. Then chaos. Spraggue found himself suddenly alone, cross-legged on the gold plush carpet. Act One, scene three! He leafed feverishly through the blue-bound script, found the scene, relaxed. Dr. John Seward made no appearance until the second act. He was of England, not Transylvania. Act One was Transylvania; he should have remembered that.

He sat in the first row and closed his eyes. With actors, half the game was guessing *when* they lied, half *why*. Seldom *whether*. A life spent reciting other people's words made lying too damn easy.

Act One, scene three. Dramatis Personae: the brides of Dracula. That would be Georgina and the dark-haired Deirdre. Jonathan Harker: tall, blond Greg Hudson, a man with an effeminate air—until he looked at Emma Healey. Dracula himself: John Langford. Spraggue settled back in his seat. Years since he'd seen Langford act. The man was magic. A matinee-idol profile did him no harm, but he had more than that, some animal magnetism that made the audience *care* about him, hero or villain. Which would his Dracula be?

Onstage, Jonathan Harker, the English solicitor, slept, his elegant body stretched out on a chaise in the vampire's library. Yes, that scene; Spraggue remembered the plot. Harker had been cautioned by the Count never to sleep in any room other than his own bedchamber. But worn out by the exertions of attempted escape from the castle, the lawyer had disobeyed. It was night now. Enter the brides of Dracula.

The women approached the sleeping man.

"He was warned," said the brunette. She laughed and the laugh was hauntingly evil.

27

"And *we* were warned," added Georgina, hesitantly. Her face was cunning. She wanted the man. But something frightened her.

Her dark companion licked her sharp white teeth. "We have obeyed. The master will have nothing to complain of."

"Then you shall kiss him first," said Georgina. "Yours is the right to begin."

On the chaise, Harker opened his eyes and stared at the approaching brides, enthralled.

The women came closer. Deirdre broke the silence. "He's young and strong. There's blood enough for two."

As she spoke, she leaned over Harker and kissed him full on the lips. Georgina gave a low growl. The transformation from women to beasts was well done—clear, but subtle enough to stay within the bounds of possibility. Shocking, but not laugh-producing. Deirdre growled in answer, raised her long neck, bared her teeth for the kill.

Dracula was in the room without entering. A trick of lighting or a trapdoor? Or was it just that Spragg's attention was so completely absorbed by the scene at stage right that the stage-left movement hadn't caught his eye?

Langford wore black. Not a costume. The dark turtleneck and slacks wouldn't attract a second look on the street. It was the man inside. He wore the nondescript garments with flair. On him, they were costume. He'd probably worn nothing but black for weeks in preparation for the role, Spragg thought. Langford had a reputation for being scrupulous about detail. But had his eyebrows always been so black and shaggy? His skin so pale? His cheekbones so prominent? How much makeup and how much sheer acting ability?

No matter. He was Dracula. At the sound of his voice the women froze. He grabbed Deirdre by the neck. His slight motion threw her across the room.

"How dare you touch him? How dare you look at him when I had forbidden it?"

Georgina cowered as the vampire raged. The dark woman confronted him.

She laughed, a cold hollow sound. "What would you have us do? Starve? Ignore the beauty of human men? We're not like you. You never loved."

"You never love," echoed the blonde.

The Vampire King softened. He crossed the room, took the women in his arms. "I, too, can love. You know it from the past." He knelt, blond Georgina on his knee, Deirdre in the crook of his right arm. He whispered, "I promise you, when I am done with him you shall kiss him at your will. But for now, go. I have work to do tonight."

"And are we to have nothing, then?" pouted Deirdre.

Georgina gave a little squeal and pointed. On the floor, near the place where Dracula had first appeared, was a sack. The two women pounced on it eagerly, transforming themselves again into animals, bacchantes. Deirdre, eyes gleaming, reached in the bag to pull the morsel out.

A human child, Spraggue remembered.

Deirdre screamed, a shriek that was female, not animal. The sack hit the stage floor with a thud. The dark woman held up her hands. Blood trickled down to her elbows.

"What the—" Darien's yell was almost lost in the commotion. Spraggue found himself onstage. He grabbed the bag that had fallen from Deirdre's unresisting fingers.

"It's not the doll," she whispered. "It's something awful. Look at my hands." She stared at them, transfixed.

"Georgie," Spraggue said firmly. "Go help her wash up."

Georgina gawked. The stage manager propelled Deirdre offstage.

Spraggue eyed the sack warily. Darien was beside him now. The others circled, waiting: Greg, Langford, Eddie, Emma, Georgina. Spraggue wished he could see their faces more clearly.

At first he thought the thing in the bag was a skull. His hand recoiled as he touched it. Too flimsy for bone. He lifted it out. The light caught it and Greg Hudson gasped.

The head was a likeness of Hudson's. Grotesquely thin, a caricature, but unmistakably him. The neck had been rudely hacked from a nonexistent body. The straw-blond wig, partially askew, was dappled with blood from the gaping wound. The face itself was beautifully sculpted. A Halloween mask attached to a wig form, Spraggue hazarded. The whole thing covered with celastic strips, molded to Greg's image. Whoever the joker was, he—or she—had an artist's touch.

A retching sound came from Hudson's direction. He ran offstage. Emma followed. Everyone started to speak at once.

Spraggue paid no attention to the tumult. He'd seen something else inside the sack. A flash of white, stiff cardboard with rough penciled numbers. Familiar printing that made him think of Mickey Mouse paper and decapitated bats.

In the confusion, he transferred the card to his pocket. It didn't say much: 1538. That was it.

With luck, Spraggue thought, he'd have the whole thing figured out by the time the show played its one thousand, five hundred and thirty-eighth performance.

Chapter Five

The next evening, Spraggue ate sushi alone at the Japanese restaurant down the block from the theater. The meal was good. Not great, the way his Thursday night dinners customarily were. Thursday night meant dinner at the Brookline estate—created by Dora, the cook who'd spoiled Spraggue for Boston's best restaurants.

But not tonight. He'd called Aunt Mary filled with excuses and finally agreed to come over later for a nightcap. No time was too late for Aunt Mary.

He savored the delicately flavored raw fish slowly, then abandoned his chopsticks, finished his green tea, and ordered a refill on the small flask of saki.

Rehearsal had gone like clockwork. No bloody heads, no decapitated bats. Just nine straight hours of lines, cues, and blocking, with costume fittings and publicity stills sandwiched in between.

Eight-thirty. Fifteen more minutes and it would be dark enough to begin. Rehearsal had broken up at six. The crew left at seven. Some of the cast had stopped for a drink at the bar next door. Spraggue had watched them from his carefully chosen dining nook. Everyone was gone now.

He fingered the picklocks in his left hip pocket and smiled. How close he'd come to giving them to a police-sergeant friend after he'd decided that private detection was not for him. He'd convinced himself that he must have thrown them away, right until the moment he'd found them in the bottom desk drawer.

Spraggue paid the check, bowed to the impossibly tiny waitress, and left. Two minutes' walking brought him back to the theater.

The side door was the best bet, opening off an unfrequented

alley. The chief danger would be muggers, not an overzealous police force.

His technique was a little rusty after years of legal keys. Patience. Slow, careful work would avoid those tiny marks around the keyhole, surefire indicators of a "B & E." A minute passed like ten, then the door creaked and Spraggue was inside.

The side door brought him into a long passageway near the costume shop. Storage rooms on his left gave off a musty odor. He stood still, waiting until his eyes adjusted to the blackness. Then quietly, on rubber soles, he made his way down the corridor toward the stage.

The hallway ran straight for twenty yards, then branched. To the right, a short passage led to the paint room and a stairway down to the dressing rooms. The stage was straight ahead, hidden behind double doors. Spraggue turned left. Darien's office was upstairs.

He heard a muffled voice and stopped dead. Someone was on-stage. A person with a key, a right to be there? The stage manager? Or the joker.

Six steps brought him back to the double doors. He turned the knob slowly, opened the right-hand door a crack.

The work lights were on, the curtain down. Deirdre, the tall brunette bride of Dracula, was alone, rehearsing a scene. She turned, sank into a hard wooden chair as if it were a comfortable Victorian love seat, and continued her dialogue:

"Oh, John, you do understand, don't you? I'm sorry to have worried you."

She paused, heard a flattering response, and replied: "I'm glad, my darling. So glad. Don't fret about me anymore. I'll be fine. It's only these dreams, John. Such bad dreams. . . ."

It was an attractive performance, unassuming. Childlike and womanly at the same time. Confiding, but hesitant. An interesting interpretation. But not of a vampire queen.

Spraggue cleared his throat.

"Who's there?"

"Don't worry," he said. "Michael Spraggue. I didn't realize anyone else was here."

Damn, he said inwardly. I should have.

Her pale intense face relaxed. "I didn't either. How'd you get in?"

Spraggue smiled. "How did you?"

"I just stayed. I love empty theaters at night. Especially this

32

theater. It has such wonderful vibrations. Did you know that a man killed himself here?"

"I'd heard."

"Hanged himself." Her voice played with the sound. "Right here, center stage. Such a romantic way to die. . . ."

"I doubt he thought so."

She giggled with her mouth but her eyes were far away. "Will you play a scene with me?"

"I don't have any scenes with the brides of Dracula."

"The scene I was just doing," she said. "That's one of yours."

"Mine and Lucy's, isn't it?"

"Yes. I love that scene. Right after the first attacks on Lucy. She knows she should tell you about them, but there's something so fascinating, so erotic, about the vampire that all she does is complain about her 'bad dreams.'"

"I'm afraid I don't know the scene yet," he said. How to get rid of the woman! Would she rattle on with the dreamy voice and the distant eyes all night?

"Do you believe in dreams?" Deirdre asked. "In portents?"

"Sometimes," Spraggue said carefully.

Her eyes widened, stared into nothingness. "I do. I'm only Emma's understudy, Mr. Spraggue, but I believe that I'll play Lucy. That's why I have to stay late. To rehearse. I have to be very good, very professional, when the accident happens."

"What accident?" Spraggue was almost afraid to prompt her. The woman blurted out her thoughts in a stream of consciousness. Her eyes rarely met his. She seemed to speak to an invisible presence. Not an audience, but some specific person. Maybe the vibrations of the dead Mr. Phelps. . . .

"Accident," she murmured. "Not the right word. So hard to find just the right word. *Incident.* One of our actors already left because of an *incident.* . . ."

"Frank Hodges," said Spraggue. Either Darien had been less discreet than he'd claimed or—

"And I hardly think Greg was amused by that *incident* today. I was terrified."

She seemed more entranced than terrified now, thought Spraggue. "Have there been any other 'incidents,' Deirdre?" he said.

She smiled. "Nothing to fuss about. I mean, it wasn't voodoo or anything. No hair, no nail clippings—"

"You've lost me."

"The doll in my hotel room. I think Gina got one, too."

At least someone called the blonde "Gina."

"It was in my bed," she continued. "Almost three weeks ago. Maybe the second or third day of rehearsal. Sit down and I'll tell you about it. I haven't told the others."

"Why not?"

"It wasn't funny enough to be a joke or scary enough to be a threat. It was just odd. . . . And there was never the right moment, you know. You need a mood for a tale like this one. . . ."

"An empty theater at night?"

"Exactly." She settled back in the chair, ready to begin. How much truth will I get, wondered Spraggue. How much embroidery?

"I'd gone out to eat after rehearsal, so I didn't get home until nine. It wouldn't have scared me at all if I'd come home before dark."

"Yes?" Spraggue said. Deirdre seemed to have forgotten all about him. Was she really an actress or had Darien recruited her for the part out of a local coven?

"The light was out. I turned the switch but nothing happened. Do you know the Emory Hotel?"

"No."

"It's cheap. I was sorry to leave. At the Emory, broken light switches are *de rigueur*. I tried the lamp in the corner. That was dead, too. At least the two lower bulbs were dead. The third bulb was different. Someone had rigged it all up, with a baffle and a theatrical gel—midnight blue. It was shining on the doll in my bed."

She paused. "There *was* a resemblance. The doll had long dark hair, a pale complexion. But she also had a two-inch gap between her head and her body."

Decapitation. Nice little fixation for our prankster to have, thought Spraggue. The bat, Greg's mask, now beheaded dolls. "You changed hotels." he said.

"Yes."

"Was there anything else about the doll that frightened you?"

"The head was stuffed with garlic. There were two small marks on the neck, white with red centers, just like in the script. A trickle of blood from the mouth. Fake, like today. . . . Oh, and the doll was in a rather immodest position, dress hiked, legs spread, and anatomical details added with great care. . . . There

34

was a little piece of paper stuck to the doll's breast with a toothpick type of thing. A stake right through the heart."

"Anything on the paper?"

"Just numbers, I think. Three or four different numbers. Not even threes and sevens and mystical numbers. Just regular numbers."

"A phone number, maybe? Did you save it?"

"No." She was definite about that. "Not enough numbers." She looked up. The story was finished. "What time is it?"

"Nine-fifteen. Are you late?"

"I suppose. I never wear a watch. Time is so intrusive, you know. But I like to be in bed before midnight and I do an hour of yoga before I sleep. My cat howls if I don't feed him on time. I'd better go. And I don't think you should stay here all alone."

"If you can—" Spraggue began.

"But I'm not at all afraid of ghosts, Michael Spraggue. Are you?"

"No." Spraggue kept his gaze level. "Ghosts don't bother me much."

"Not even the ghosts of suicides?"

"You mean old Phelps?"

"You know about him." Deirdre nodded approvingly. "Suicides are funny. They can just *become* vampires. No need to get bitten."

"Spontaneous vampire generation," said Spraggue gravely.

She laughed. "It's not that you're unafraid of ghosts. You just don't believe in them; that's a very different thing. If I were you, I wouldn't stay here alone tonight."

"I don't intend to stay long," Spraggue said. "Once over tomorrow's blocking and I'm gone. I'll probably catch up with you before you get on the trolley."

To his relief she picked up a jacket off a chair. "Good-bye then," she said. Her high-heeled shoes made no sound on the steps or the carpeting. She disappeared into the lobby. Spraggue heard the door swing shut. Silence.

He moved quickly. The switch that turned off the work lights was near the double doors. Thank God for that. At least he wouldn't have to wander across a pitch-black stage hoping Deirdre didn't rehearse with the trapdoors open. He climbed up the stairs to Darien's office.

The lock was old and rusty. Spraggue worked carefully with the picklocks for ten minutes before it yielded.

He pulled the shade on the window overlooking Huntington Avenue, resisting the impulse to open it and disperse the office's stuffy sick-sweet smell, before flicking on the faint overhead bulb. The desk, the sideboard, a single two-drawer file cabinet; the search shouldn't take long. Facts. He needed facts: résumés, programs, financial data. If he waited for Darien to "ascertain the propriety of releasing such documents," the damn show would be over.

The bottom drawer of the file cabinet was the bonanza. Résumés neatly filed in alphabetical order, a program mock-up on oversized cardboard sheets. The file folder marked FINANCIAL was empty.

He searched the other drawers again. Maybe Darien had taken the stuff to his hotel room to glance over. Maybe the fat house manager kept those files. By the time he got the paperwork over to the all-night photocopying place in Harvard Square, replaced the originals, had that nightcap with Aunt Mary. . . . time for rehearsal again!

He paused for a moment with his hand on the light switch. A red leather blotter lay slightly askew on the desk. He retraced his steps.

The missing file wasn't underneath. Financial records wouldn't be stuffed into a small unsealed white envelope.

Sprague straightened the blotter, then lifted it again. The printing, that's what was familiar. There was more to go on here; this letter had been through the mail. Three whole lines of letters and numbers in penciled block caps. Not just a name, not just a few numbers. . . .

Sprague slid the letter out of the envelope, spread it on the desktop. This one was easy to understand, too:

MR. DARIEN, the letter read. IS ONE SUICIDE ENOUGH FOR THIS THEATRE??? ENCORE!!!

Sprague wrinkled his nose. The room's odor seemed suddenly stronger. He crouched. Near the wastebasket, it was almost unbearable.

Using the tips of his fingers, staying an arm's length away, he tossed aside a few discarded sheets of paper.

The bird was large, black, and dead. No signs of violence on it. Terrible stink, all the same.

At least, Sprague thought, it's not an albatross.

Chapter Six

A dark slim silhouette decorated the cover page of the program, a three-quarter back view of a man enveloped in black velvet. The long cape swirled fantastically into a border design. To the right of the figure, in bold, black caps, the title, *Dracula*. Underneath, in elegant script: "Directed by Arthur Darien."

"I like it," Sprague's Aunt Mary said. "Very Aubrey Beardsley."

Sprague turned the page. The cast list was next, in order of appearance:

JONATHAN HARKER	Gregory Hudson
COUNT DRACULA	John Langford
THE BRIDES OF DRACULA	Deirdre Marten
	Gina Phillips
RENFIELD	Edward Lafferty
DR. JOHN SEWARD	Frank Hodges
MINA MURRAY	Caroline Ambrose
LUCY WESTENRA	Emma Healey
DR. ABRAHAM VAN HELSING	Gustave Grayling

Sprague let his eyes close while his aunt pored over the list, shutting out the vast proportions of the balconied, two-story library of the old Sprague house. Even the Cézanne over the marble fireplace offered no relief to exhaustion-blurred eyes. What time was it? One o'clock? Two? Never too late for Aunt Mary.

He grinned at the back of her variegated head. She had hoped for a smooth transition, a graceful fading from red to silver. But the process seemed to have halted halfway, leaving untidy patches of both colors. Oddly enough, it suited her perfectly.

"Well?" she said, her clear voice belying her sixty-seven years.

Spraggue took a long sip of syrupy amber wine, a '59 Beerenauslese Aunt Mary had brought up from the cellar to celebrate his new job. He smiled his appreciation. Mary tapped the cast list sharply with a painted fingernail.

"That," said Spraggue hastily, "minus one, plus one, is the list of suspects."

"Who's out?"

"Frank Hodges. I've got his part. He could have been playing the tricks up until last week, but he had nothing to do with today's games. Definitely in New York. I spoke to him on the phone. He wished me luck."

"Did you tell him you were investigating the—"

"No. Things like that have a way of getting around. I called to humbly ask him for any character insight he might offer me on Dr. John Seward. I had a hard time getting him off the line."

Aunt Mary crossed off Hodges's name. "And whose name gets added?"

"Don't scrawl it on the cast list. She's crew. The stage manager. Woman named Karen Snow."

"Nice name."

"Seems a nice person," said Spraggue shortly.

"What about the rest of the crew?"

"Darien says they're out. There's a fat guy named Dennis, the house manager. I'd like to know more about him. But Darien assures me he's out of the running."

"And how reliable is Mr. Darien?" asked Aunt Mary mildly.

Spraggue yawned. "How reliable is anyone in this business?"

"What I meant was, is he drinking?"

Spraggue's eyebrow went up again. "You know about that?"

"Doesn't everyone? Don't you remember that business with the auto crash? The Boston papers hardly touched it, but the New York press went after Darien with a vengeance."

"An accident—" Spraggue said, dredging up bits and pieces of the story from his memory.

"A woman was killed. I don't recall the name. An actress, I think. Unknown."

"And Darien was charged?"

"No," Aunt Mary said positively. "The public prosecutor wanted to go for vehicular homicide. Said Darien was drunk. He so often was at that time. But someone slipped up. I forget. Either no breathalyzer test was given or the results were lost or tampered with. A police officer lost his job over the mixup. Darien got off with bruises and bad press."

"As far as I know, Darien's stone-cold sober." Sprague pulled a folded scrap of paper out of his pocket. "But even if he isn't drinking now, this could encourage him to start."

He handed a facsimile of the note he'd found on Darien's desk to his aunt. "It came attached to a dead bird."

She fingered the note thoughtfully. "Whose suicide does this refer to?"

"Samuel Borgmann Phelps."

"Ah."

"You knew him?"

"*Of* him. When I was a teenager, attending a performance at Phelps's Boston Rep was *the* thing to do. He held the most marvelous parties, right up until the end. Thought he'd turn Boston into Broadway. No one knew how badly off he really was. The family had generations of wealth behind it. Or so everyone thought."

"What happened to them?"

"The Phelps family? I don't know. He had children, I'm sure. There was a huge turnout at the funeral. Would you like me to find out?"

"I can—"

"I would like to help, Michael. And I do enjoy snooping. One of the few vocations eminently suited to the elderly."

"Well, I could use someone to do a résumé check. See if these folks have all done what they've claimed."

"Wonderful." Aunt Mary beamed. "And what about money, Michael? Who has a major financial interest in Darien's success or failure? He's no Sam Phelps; he can't handle everything on his own. I could ask around Massachusetts Council of Arts membership, a sound credit rating, a reputation as an eccentric, and dithery ways go far when asking impertinent questions."

"Terrific." Sprague smiled at his anything-but-dithery aunt. "I'll keep my eye on the cast. If my eye will stay open."

"Early rehearsal tomorrow?"

"Two-one, Two-two, and Two-three. All scenes I yak my head off in."

"Don't drive back to Cambridge then," Mary said earnestly. "The tower room is always ready for you here. Dora cherishes the thought that someday you'll get fed up with your own cooking and move back."

39

"If I ever do, it'll be for Dora's strawberry tarts."

"Seriously, Michael, it is your house—"

"And you live in it for me. It's too damn big, Mary. I'm uncomfortable here. We've been through this—"

Aunt Mary rang the bell on the desk top. Pierce ushered Spraggue out, wished him a safe drive. The butler refused to respond to Spraggue's wink. Sometimes the dignity of his position overcame the memories of the hide-and-seek games he had played with Michael many years before.

Spraggue drove home at a leisurely speed. The wine had left him relaxed, a little high. To pass the time, he recited his lines, enjoying the baritone echo in the small space. Act Two, scene one finished. Now Two-two. Then Two-three. Numbers.

He pulled the car off to the side of Hammond Street, flicked on the dome light. Then he began to fumble methodically through his pockets. The note, Greg's note in the bloody sack. What were the numbers?

He found it finally, carefully placed in his wallet. Yes. Four numbers—one Roman, three Arabic. The first one, Roman: that would be the act number. Then the scene. Then the line. Act One, scene five, line thirty-eight.

Spraggue's fingers scrabbled through the blue-bound *Dracula* script. Act One. Act one, scene two. Scene three. He flipped the page, stopped, turned back.

He was wrong. *Dracula* had no fifth scene in the first act.

He drove the rest of the way home in silence.

Chapter Seven

For the fourth time in two minutes, Darien glared at his wristwatch.

"I've called his apartment twice, Mr. Darien," Karen Snow said. "No answer." She hesitated, then added, "Look, he only lives a few blocks from here. I could walk over and—"

"I'm sure you have a great deal of work to do here!" said Darien loudly. "Technical rehearsal tomorrow. Don't tell me you can spare the time! If Eddie Lafferty isn't ready to go onstage in ten minutes, we'll rehearse with his understudy. And make sure Lafferty is fined!"

"Arthur—" The stage manager's voice was soft, but the protest was there.

"It's his business to be here! What's the matter with you, Karen?"

The stage manager's face became stonier than ever. Only her mouth moved as she snapped, "I'm worried. Eddie's never been a minute late before. With all the weird events around here. . . ." Her voice trailed off.

"Karen's been like a sister to Eddie," Georgina said quietly. She and Spraggue sat five rows behind and slightly to the right of Arthur Darien, waiting for rehearsal to proceed. "He's the baby of the company. Karen showed him the ropes."

"At least that's what *he* says," interrupted Greg Hudson. "It's *my* opinion that older sister, for one, is ripe for a little incest!"

"Be quiet, Greg!" Georgina's cheeks flamed. "Do you want her to hear you?"

"I really don't care," Hudson said calmly, and walked away. Hit and run, that was Hudson's style, thought Spraggue.

Georgina let out her breath soundlessly, watching Karen. The argument over Eddie continued; the stage manager couldn't

41

have overheard. "Sometimes I think Greg's crazy!" she said, moving closer to Spraggue. "He seems to want to hurt everybody—"

"Do you think he's the company joker?"

"No," she said swiftly. "I'm sure he's not."

"Why?"

"Not the type. He lets all his nasty feelings out. Wouldn't you think that the kind of person who'd do things like that would be—well, all quiet and polite on the outside?"

"And dark and twisted inside?"

Georgina nodded gravely. "Yes. Sick and mad. . . . To play such cruel jokes—"

"He's done something to you." Spraggue kept his voice light but firm. If there were no question, there would be no denial.

"Yes," she murmured. The memory of the beheaded doll clouded her gray eyes.

"Deirdre told me about the doll," Spraggue said.

"She did?" Georgina stared at her fingernails.

"Why didn't you say anything about it?"

She kept her head down and answered lamely but doggedly. "It wasn't the kind of thing I wanted to talk about. . . ."

"You might have told Darien."

"What could he do? It was over. I wanted to forget it ever happened."

"Georgie, was there a piece of paper stuck to the doll?"

She looked up finally. "Yes."

"Do you still have it?"

"I might."

"Do me a favor."

She smiled at his pleading. "Okay."

"Lunch break. Go get the paper. Don't tell anybody else about it. Don't mention where you're going."

"But, Michael—"

"Spraggue!" Darien's voice shot across the rows of seats.

"Yes."

"Come here!"

Spraggue gave Georgina's cold hand a squeeze. "Don't forget," he said. Georgina's eyes avoided his, but her hand squeezed back. He walked rapidly over to Darien.

Karen Snow's dark, angry eyes were still fastened on the director. He seemed flustered, but kept command of his voice. "I wondered, Spraggue," he began meekly. " *We* wondered if you'd mind going over to Lafferty's place and taking a look around.

42

Just to hoist him out of bed, I expect." Darien tried a laugh. It fell flat. He raised his voice; the rest of the conversation was for Georgina's curious ears. "I thought you'd be the best person to send. All your Act Two scenes are with Eddie, so I can't very well rehearse you without him. And Karen has volunteered to go over your blocking tomorrow night, if that's okay—so any time we miss can be made up. I can work the women's scenes while you're gone—"

Maybe he'd go on talking forever, Spraggue thought. He stopped the anxious voice with a word. "Sure," he said easily. "Just give me an address."

"One hundred forty-one Hemenway," said Karen. "Apartment 5."

She hadn't left Darien's side to look it up. Too quick a response for an "older sister"?

"You take a left out the front door, then a right at the corner," she said.

"I know where it is." Spraggue turned and left.

Does she know about me? he wondered as he walked the few blocks to Eddie's apartment. Had she suggested to Darien that he send me? Her dark eyes were intelligent, hard to read. She had a way of using them to close people out; her eyes were shields, hard and opaque. Maybe he could break them down during the extra blocking rehearsal. She'd be a good ally. If she wasn't the joker.

Whatever he was getting paid, Eddie Lafferty wasn't squandering it on rent. One hundred forty-one Hemenway was ugly yellow brick, a narrow five stories high, flanked on either side by fragrant alleys. The building to the right was a burned-out hulk. The street-level windows were haphazardly boarded over with plywood.

The neighborhood wasn't exactly quiet. Rock blared from an open window across the street. Voices called from the Laundromat on the corner. Usual day-to-day noises. No wailing police sirens. Whatever had happened to Eddie, at least it didn't rate that. Or, thought Spraggue, maybe it just hadn't been discovered yet.

Up three crumbling cements steps. A scrawled yellowed notice advised callers to ring and wait for the buzzer. Spraggue tried the door; it swung open at his touch. Some security.

Apartment five. He climbed two flights of narrow steps.

Spraggue wasted three seconds trying Eddie's door. Considering the ease of entry downstairs, each apartment probably boasted five or six locks—chains, deadbolts, anything to soothe the fear.

He knocked, expecting no reply. The picklocks were already active in his hands when he heard it: a low moan followed by a sharp crash.

"Eddie?" Spraggue called.

Again the moaning, grunting noise.

Spraggue made short work of the feeble main lock. There were no chains or bolts. He entered quickly, closing the door behind him.

The room was dark and stuffy; heavy curtains obscured the windows. Spraggue took a step, kicked something hard but insubstantial. It skittered across the floor. His hands searched the wall to the left of the door, found the light switch, clicked it on.

Later, he noticed the slit pillows, overturned furniture, tumbled-out drawers. Later, he had time to read the scrawled inscriptions on the walls. At first, all he saw was Eddie.

A pajama-clad Eddie Lafferty balanced precariously on tiptoe on a chair near the center of the room. His mouth was gagged. His blue eyes stared wildly. His hands were tied behind his back. There was a noose around his neck. The rope stretched up over a pipe running the length of the room. It was tied off taut on a closet handle.

Lafferty stared at him blankly, then his eyes rolled up and he started to sag. Spraggue opened his pocket knife as he sprang across the room. He cut the rope with one hand, broke Eddie's fall with the other.

He eased the limp body down to the floor, removed the gag. He pushed Lafferty over on his side and untied his hands. The rope yielded easily. His hand closed over Lafferty's wrist. Pulse fast and faint. Spraggue dodged debris and found the tiny kitchen, ran cold water from the tap into two glasses. One he poured over Eddie. He drank half the other then offered it to the still spluttering actor.

"You're all right, Eddie," he said soothingly, seeing the wildness come back into the huge eyes. "It's all over."

"My God." The boy's voice was a feeble croak.

Spraggue grabbed a cushion that had lost its chair and shoved it under Eddie's head. "Better?"

Eddie tried a tremulous smile. His lips shook.

"Can you tell me what happened?"

"More water."

44

Spraggue held the glass for him. A lot of it dribbled to the floor.

"What time is it?" Eddie asked.

"Eleven thirty-five."

"My God," Eddie said again.

"How long have you been perched up there?"

"I don't know. I was still asleep when he came in."

"Who came in?" said Spraggue.

"Something. I was asleep and something hauled me out of bed. It was dark."

"A man or a woman?"

"I couldn't tell. I couldn't—" Eddie gulped, raised his hands to his Adam's apple. "My throat hurts," he said fuzzily.

"I know," said Spraggue. "Whisper, but try to answer."

"It had a black face, a black cloak, black gloves. It was all black, like a shadow. . . ."

"He wore a mask?"

Eddie's eyes lit up. "Maybe. A ski mask. All black."

"Did you see the eyes, Eddie? What color eyes?"

"I don't know. Dark, I think. The room was so blurry. . . . I didn't have my glasses."

"Height?"

"Average. I don't know. At first I was in bed. Then I had to climb on the chair—"

"Voice. Male or female?"

"It whispered, Spraggue. The cloak hid the body. Strong, though. Whoever it was. Powerful."

"Did he knock you out?"

Eddie gave a tiny half-smile. "He *or* she. No. I did what he said. He had a gun. I'm not brave. He tied my hands. He made me stick my head through the noose. I had to stand on tiptoe." Eddie's voice quavered, almost stopped. "I thought I was going to die. . . ."

"Take it easy. It's all over," Spraggue said.

"Then he threw everything around the room."

"Wouldn't somebody hear?"

"Around here?" Eddie's voice was bitter. "People hear plenty in a neighborhood like this. They stay alive ignoring it."

"What did he do then?"

"He wrote on the walls. Then he just stood and looked at me. I thought he was going to kick the chair over. He laughed, a whispery kind of noise, but a laugh. He said: 'I have a message for you.' It was a bunch of numbers. It didn't make any sense. He

45

told me to memorize it, made me repeat it. I can't remember it at all now."

"Let me know if it comes back."

"Then he left."

"Does the door lock automatically, Eddie?"

"Yes."

"How did he get in?"

"I don't know. I didn't see."

"You don't use the chain when you're inside?"

"No."

The door hadn't been hard to force. He'd have to check it for signs of recent tampering.

Eddie caught his hand. "I just stood there, Spraggue. I was so scared I'd fall. I kept trying to get my hands free; I figured that was my only hope. I almost did."

Spraggue glanced at Eddie's wrists. Rope burns, abrasions. He was telling the truth.

"That chair." Eddie nodded at the black wooden job, knocked on its side. "I could reach it with my foot. If I heard anyone on the stairs I was going to kick it over, hope somebody would notice. But no one came by. I kicked it when I heard you knock. I almost lost my balance."

So that was the crash he had heard.

"Do you have ice in the freezer?" Spraggue asked.

"Yes," said Eddie. "I guess I'm trying to say thank you."

"You're welcome. I think you would have gotten your hands loose in time."

"I'm glad I didn't have to."

Spraggue emptied an ice tray into a frayed kitchen towel, wrapped it into a long cylinder, and gave it to Eddie. "Put that around your throat," he said.

The phone rang.

"It's been ringing all morning—"

Spraggue picked up the receiver.

"Spraggue?" It was Karen Snow.

"Put Darien in a cab and get him over here," said Spraggue.

"Eddie?"

"He's all right." Spraggue could hear the sigh of relief, felt irrationally displeased by it.

"Can I talk to him?" she asked.

"No. Later."

"Darien's rehearsing. He's not going to like it."

46

"Get him here in ten minutes or he might not have anything to rehearse. Okay?"

"Okay," she said. The phone went dead.

Eddie was sitting up, the towel clutched to his throat. His color was better. He looked at Spraggue and managed a grin.

"Don't bother talking," Spraggue said shortly. "Go over the whole incident in your mind, see it again. Do it like an acting exercise, one sense at a time. Maybe you can get those numbers back."

Eddie nodded.

Spraggue searched the room. It was a shambles, a useless mess. What to look for? A button off a long dark cloak? A fingerprint left by a gloved hand? Somehow his eyes kept coming back to the writing on the walls. That familiar printing, those unevenly scrawled black caps. Carefully uneven, planned sloppiness—the person who'd created that mask of Greg Hudson could do a far neater job. Spraggue sniffed at the gooey letters, scraped some of the gunk off on a fingernail. Lipstick. Deep, blood red.

A female? No. Actors were comfortable with lipstick, men and women. And no clue to the prankster's height. The inscription ran all around the room at different levels, sometimes skirting the floorboards, sometimes almost at ceiling height. He must have used a chair—and an entire tube of lipstick.

The message, though, never varied. CANCEL THE SHOW. CANCEL THE SHOW. CANCEL THE SHOW; it said over and over.

Chapter Eight

Arthur Darien decided against the police. Buoyed by Darien's concern and his offer to pay all damages, Eddie went along with him. Spraggue called them anyway, dialing a number three years hadn't made him forget.

The pay phone on the corner of Huntington Avenue was in typical shape: door kicked in, phone book ripped out. But it had two advantages: it commanded a view of the front door of the theater, and was far enough from that front door so that no one entering or leaving the theater could overhear Spraggue's end of the conversation.

Lieutenant Detective Fred Hurley grabbed the phone on the first ring. "Hurley. Records," he snarled.

"Charming as always," said Spraggue.

"Huh?"

"Did you happen to find an envelope on your desk this morning?"

"Yeah, but I figured I was seeing things 'cause the guy that sent me the envelope, I haven't seen him for years. Is that you, Spraggue?"

"You don't recognize my voice?"

"After all these years? Christ!"

"Can you help me out?"

"You back in the business, Spraggue?"

"No. Just a little thing I'm handling for a friend."

"Some little thing. Must be ten names in that envelope."

"Eleven. All I want is a rundown, anybody with a record. I listed birthplaces and last known addresses. That should help."

"You're all heart. Look, I'm busy, but I'll try."

"Just charge a little of that overtime to me instead of the city. That's all I'm asking."

Hurley's voice took on a new note. "You going to tell me who you're working for?"

"No harm in that. I'm acting again, for Arthur Darien, over at the Fens Theater."

"Over by Symphony, right? Old District 4. Interesting."

"Why?" Spraggue asked. Hurley's brain was like a camera. Once it photographed information, the image stayed put. That was the department's excuse for sticking the former homicide specialist at a desk in Records.

"You help me, I help you, right?" said Hurley.

"Right."

"Then keep your eyes open. That area's very intriguing to your local police force."

"You have to tell me what to keep my eye on, Hurley. I'm just an amateur."

"Sure. Anything out of the ordinary. But especially drugs. Somebody's doing some fancy cocaine dealing around there. Neighborhood's going to hell. Burglary, arson. . . ."

"If I stumble across the odd kilo, I'll dump it at your door."

"I'll owe you for anything that helps get me out of this crummy desk job. Those other two items you want are going to take me some time. The accident report from New York and that Chicago business—"

"Probably just gossip-column fodder, but I'd appreciate it if you'd get me a copy of the death certificate."

"Geoffrey Ambrose, huh?"

"Right."

"Like I said, I'll try. Call me in a couple days."

"I'll call you tomorrow, Fred."

"Great. I love to talk. But don't expect anything until at least the day after. I can't tell the cops that I'm holding up their stuff just to do you a favor, you know."

"Talk to you tomorrow, Fred." Spraggue hung up.

Outside the theater a limousine halted, tooted its horn twice. John Langford, swathed in a shapeless black cloak, wearing huge dark glasses, descended the theater stairs at a regal pace. The uniformed chauffeur got out of the car and opened the rear street-side door.

But the limo didn't move. It disrupted traffic on Huntington Avenue for the next few minutes. Then red-haired Emma appeared on the front steps, ran swiftly downstairs, and vanished into the car. The limo took off, just catching the tail end of the yellow at the intersection, and roared out of sight.

Spraggue left the phone booth and strolled back to the theater to find Georgina Phillips.

She was in her dressing room, eyes closed, feet propped up on the ledge that served as a makeup table. Spraggue was willing to bet that Georgina rated a private room only because no one else would put up with dressing in a closet. The cubicle reminded him of the phone booth he'd just vacated. Standing dead center, he could touch all four walls without stretching.

Georgina had tried to make the phone booth livable. The far wall boasted a Sierra Club poster, framed to imitate the window the room sadly lacked. A paper lantern attempted to soften the glare from the bare bulb on the ceiling. Photographs covered up some of the peeling plaster. One was probably Georgina as a child. Hair ruffled, slender body hunched in sleep, she looked much the same now.

She must have sensed his presence. Her eyes opened and she smiled. "What are you thinking?"

"Oh, something like, 'There's no art to find the mind's construction in the face—'"

"Stop it!" Georgina sat up angrily. "That's from *Macbeth*! You should know better than to quote the Scottish play in a theater, of all places!"

"I forgot," Spraggue said. "I never really believed in—"

"Some of us do."

"I'm sorry. I won't do it again."

Her eyes narrowed slightly. "You were probably thinking I looked dumb, and now I've just proved it."

"Pretty. I was thinking you looked pretty."

"Same thing, huh? Men equate 'pretty' and 'blonde' with 'dumb' in these parts, or haven't you noticed?"

"I've noticed," Spraggue said, "but it's another thing I don't believe in. I was wondering if you could help me."

Georgina shook her head, grinned ruefully. "Want to start over? I'm sorry. I guess you scared me. I woke up and there you were, towering over me. . . ."

"Forget it."

"Want to talk in the lounge? It's kind of cramped in here."

"Let's go for a walk," Spraggue said.

"So nobody'll overhear us?" Georgina whispered.

Spraggue nodded solemnly. Georgina's gray eyes gleamed. She maintained a dignified silence until they marched down the front steps of the theater. Then she looked around carefully before murmuring: "I found the stuff you wanted."

With effort, Spraggue kept a straight face. She was playing a part from an old Hitchcock movie. "Yes?" he said.

"Four-two-five-one."

"How was it written?"

She bit her lower lip in concentration. "The four was like Roman numerals, a capital i and a capital v. Then the rest all in normal numbers. No spaces anywhere."

Just like the other message.

"Does it mean something?" Georgina asked eagerly. "Do you know what it means?"

"Suggest anything to you?"

"I was thinking of playing it as my lottery number. Wait! How about a phone number? Is there any exchange that could be IV2? Just a minute!" She dove into the phone booth on the corner. "I is 4! V is 8! Is there a 482 exchange in Boston?"

"No. And you're two digits short." Georgina deflated. "But it was a fine idea," Spraggue said.

"Four-two-fifty-one." She was off again. "I-V-twenty-five-one. It's a clue, right? A message. . . ."

"Could be."

"What good's a message if nobody can understand it?"

"Exactly," Spraggue said. "That's why I think it must be something fairly obvious. At first I thought it was the play—act, scene, and line. Actors would be sure to understand that."

"Act, scene, and line! That's good, Michael. It works. Even the Roman numerals."

"Except," Spraggue said glumly, "that it doesn't. Look at your number. Starts with four. How many acts are there in *Dracula*?"

"Three."

"Right."

"Then it's probably a five-act play," Georgina said, "the one the messages are about."

"That narrows it down." He kept the sarcasm out of his voice.

"I'll think about it, Michael. I've got to get back."

"Thanks."

"And I won't say anything to anyone! 'Bye." She turned and offered him a flashing grin. "I just hope it's not *Macbeth*!"

Spraggue checked the time, turned, and crossed the street. Two blocks down, he entered a small secondhand bookshop.

"Plays?" said the elderly proprietor. "On your left, at the back of the store. Don't get so much call for them anymore. Anything special?"

"Shakespeare."

"Plenty of him. Second shelf from the bottom. Soon as the kids finish off reading him in school, they sell the books back to me."

Sprague found a tattered copy of *The Complete Tragedies,* fumbled through it until he located *Macbeth.*

"Four-twenty-five-one," he mumbled to himself. Act Four, scene twenty-five—No. Not even Shakespeare had twenty-five scenes to the act. Scene two, line fifty-one.

He found it quickly, running a finger down the yellowed page.

"And must they all be hanged that swear and lie?"

Line 51, Macduff's son to Lady Macduff. Her answer: "Every one."

Hanged. Like Eddie in his vandalized room. Like Samuel Borgmann Phelps in his beautiful bankrupt playhouse . . .

Sprague thumbed quickly through the pages. What was that other number? The one in Greg's sack. 1538. Act One this time. Scene five. Yes, Act One was a long one, seven scenes. Line 38:

> "The raven himself is hoarse
> That croaks the fatal entrance of Duncan
> Under my battlements."

A raven . . . a raven. A big black bird like the one in Darien's office. . . .

Sprague paid three dollars for the dog-eared volume and hurried back to the theater.

Chapter Nine

At first Spraggue wasn't sure he'd get along with Karen Snow.

He was five minutes late for their private, Saturday-night session, preoccupied. Even though the joker hadn't disrupted the day's rehearsal, Spraggue was just about ready to go along with the handwriting on Eddie's wall: cancel the show. At least until he'd traced every actor's performing history vis-à-vis *Macbeth*. Karen was waiting, clearly impatient. She wore the same dark slacks and T-shirt she'd had on all day. He wondered if she ever took a break, if she'd eaten lunch or dinner.

"Sorry," he said, taking the six steps up from the auditorium to the stage in two bounds.

"I didn't have anything better to do," she answered drily, setting aside her clipboard and getting to her feet.

"I know how busy you must be—" Spraggue added apologetically.

"And that's why you're late," she finished for him.

Spraggue shrugged. He wasn't about to grovel twice for a few lousy minutes. The stage manager had a glint in her dark eyes, but whether it signified suppressed humor or anger he couldn't tell. The woman's impassive face gave little away.

She pushed him through his scenes like a football coach bent on impressing a raw recruit. She was no actress, but she gave his cues intelligently in a warm, low voice. She knew her stuff; she had crosses and counters timed to the second, especially those that coincided with technical effects.

After an hour and a half, she granted him a five-minute break, adding a grudging "Not bad" and a thin secretive smile that Spraggue decided he'd like to see more of.

He glanced sorrowfully at the straight-backed prop chairs and stretched out on the hard stage floor, regretting the line-

55

memorization binge that had cost him most of the previous night's sleep. Karen kept on working. Spraggue listened to her footsteps off in the wings, counted the clicks and bangs as she moved things about. She mumbled to herself and checked off items on her ever-present clipboard.

Spraggue stared up at the roof of the stage some three stories overhead. The sensation was of lying in a fireplace, gazing up the shaft of the chimney. A vast chimney: sixty, seventy feet wide, thirty feet long. At the very top, he could barely see the crisscrossed metal of the gridiron. The space just below the grid was crowded; lighting bars crammed with instruments and cables alternated with chunks of scenery. Eight suspension battens divided the space, each batten a long iron pipe running the width of the stage. Tied to each pipe, faintly rustling in the air currents, a part of the set hung down. Spraggue identified a rocky tower from Castle Dracula, a glimmering chandelier from Dr. Seward's sitting room.

"Watch out!" Spraggue gasped, and sat up even as he spoke. The crystal chandelier had descended a good five feet before stopping with a jerk that set its beads jangling.

"Sorry." Karen's voice was muffled by the yards of drapery that separated the wings from the stage. "Just checking the counterweights."

"Isn't there some customary warning cry before you dump the lamp on my body? 'Fore' or something?"

Karen's laugh floated through the curtains. "We say 'Heads' in the theater. Short for 'Heads up.' Remember?"

"Yeah," Spraggue said. "Good posture is so important right before you get smacked in the face."

"I wouldn't worry about it. If one of these ropes breaks, you won't even have a chance to yell."

"Comforting."

"Don't fret." Karen emerged from the wings and sprawled next to Spraggue on the floor. "The rope is two-thousand-pound test-weight stuff. Not cheap. This theater has one of the best counterweight systems I've ever seen."

"Then why did the chandelier slip?"

"Improperly weighted. I released the rope clamp. If the weight on the carriage—"

"The carriage?"

"That thing backstage that looks like stacks of bullion in a bank vault. The weight on the carriage is supposed to equal the

56

weight suspended from the batten. If it does, then no movement. The chandelier was a little underbalanced, that's all."

Spraggue lay back on the wooden floor. "I think," he said, "that it might be a lot more fun to watch a performance from here. You could see all the lights glow and dim. The scenery would come closer, then fly away."

Karen leaned back on one elbow. "I've always preferred to watch the technical stuff. When I was a kid my mom kept taking me to the ballet, hoping I'd beg for dancing lessons. I couldn't take my eyes off the lights. Came home with a crick in my neck."

Spraggue wondered how anyone could put in such long hours and seem so alert. He half-expected to see dark circles under her eyes, but the skin was as pale and clear there as elsewhere. No makeup, either.

He let the companionable silence deepen before breaking it with a carefully casual question. "You know a lot about this theater?"

"Old theaters are my love."

"Tell me about this one."

She pointed. "That's where Sam Phelps died. Hanged himself from the fourth pipe. Properly weighted, too. There was some scaffolding on the stage. He climbed up, fastened the noose, and kicked the scaffolding down. It was a Saturday night. He hung there until Monday morning."

"You think he haunts the place?"

"He's supposed to put in an appearance every opening night," she said. "Seriously, no. All theaters have legends attached to them. Show people are superstitious. 'Break a leg' instead of 'good luck.' No whistling in the dressing rooms. . . ."

"Never quote *Macbeth*."

"Right."

Spraggue hesitated. "Was *Macbeth* ever performed here? Do you know?"

"Once. It wasn't successful."

"Never is. I've heard more *Macbeth* horror stories—car crashes the night before opening; chicken-pox epidemics; box-office flops."

"*Macbeth* was Samuel Phelps's last production in this theater. A disaster, critically and financially. He killed himself closing night."

"How did you know that?"

She smiled faintly. "I do my homework. I found an old book

57

on Boston theaters down at Goodspeed's. If you're curious, I'll lend it to you."

"I'm curious."

"It's downstairs." She got to her feet with a swift economy of movement.

Spraggue stood up. "I'll walk with you."

"After we get the book, we'll run your scenes again," Karen warned. "Then we'll call it a night. Okay?"

"Fine. How about ice-cream cones at Brigham's afterward?"

"No, thanks," she said stiffly.

"A drink, then? It's Saturday night in the real world."

"Just another work night for me."

"Sorry."

They stepped over a tangle of backstage cables and made their way out the double doors into the gloomy hall. Sconces, fashioned to look like Elizabethan torches, cast dim shadows on the gray stone floor.

"You keep the book in one of the dressing rooms?" Spraggue asked. Eddie's? he wondered.

"In the green room. I thought some of the actors might be interested."

Downstairs, the green room was the first door on the left. The name was traditional rather than descriptive. The green room, the actors' gathering place, was dingy battleship gray, highlighted with battered gold chintz-covered chairs and a sofa.

They found the book in one of the cupboards over the corner sink. Spraggue reached for it.

"Eddie says you saved his life," Karen said abruptly.

"Actors. They exaggerate."

"Not Eddie. It's funny; I thought I was immune to actors, but I like Eddie. Thanks for helping him."

That thin secretive smile again. Spraggue found himself hoping her immunity didn't extend to all actors. And hoping she didn't like Eddie Lafferty too much.

She interrupted his thoughts. "Do you know who did it?"

"Huh?"

"Spraggue, I know about you. I know you're not here just to act—"

"That obvious?" he asked.

The color in her cheeks deepened and she looked away. "To me, yes. I'm the one who had to get rid of the regular understudy so Darien could bring you in. I'm the stage manager. It's my job to know everything that goes on in this company."

"Congratulations. You do your job well."

"I'd rather have information than compliments. Why you? Why does Darien think you can find the joker?"

Spraggue sighed. "Once upon a time I was a private detective. Believe it or not."

"And you gave it up to play games onstage."

"I started out as an actor. RADA. Rep. Some Off-Broadway. . . ."

"Movies. You were good."

"Thanks."

"And?"

"I discovered I wasn't all that fond of actors. I developed a dislike for agents. The whole business turned me off. I'm basically nosy; I was always getting involved in stuff I had no business getting involved in. So one day I shocked my family and friends and applied for a private investigator's license."

"You didn't like it?"

"It got a little too real for me. Hurt people stayed hurt."

She nodded. "No curtain calls."

"Right."

"Did you find out anything at Eddie's?"

"No."

Her dark eyes peered into his. "Cautious. That's good, I suppose. Still, if you need any help, remember I'm always around."

Spraggue doubted he'd have any trouble remembering. "Do any of the others know why I'm here?" he asked.

"The actors?" Karen grimaced scornfully. "I doubt it. If Langford knew, he'd get appointed your deputy or take over altogether. He's our number-one busybody. The others spend every waking moment in total self-absorption."

"Still," Spraggue said, "they seem to have plenty of time to dwell on each other. John and Emma, Greg and Emma, John and Caroline Ambrose—"

"That's not affection; that's just reflected ego."

Spraggue grinned and recalled the unopened book in his hand. He checked the index quickly, riffled through the yellowed pages until he found the small section on the Fens Theater. The stage manager read over his shoulder, comfortably close.

One quarter of the first page was devoted to a faded photograph. Beady dark eyes glared from a pale wrinkled face. Hawk-nosed and thin, the lower half of his face obscured by a graying beard, Samuel Borgmann Phelps had been a striking man.

Spraggue stared at the picture, a faint memory clutching at his mind. "He looks—" he began.

At that moment, they heard the noise overhead.

"What's that?" Karen's voice sank to a whisper.

"Cleaners?"

"No."

"Stay here." Spraggue started for the door.

"No. I know this theater better than you."

"Please. It's not chauvinism, just a safety precaution. Be my backup."

She nodded. "I'll give you five minutes."

"Fine. Then bring something to hit somebody with."

"Okay."

"But not *me*."

"Do you have a gun?" she whispered.

"Never touch them."

"Here, take a flashlight. You might need it."

Spraggue turned at the door and disappeared.

At the foot of the stairs, he halted and slipped his feet out of too-new loafers. The wooden stairway was creaky enough without shoes. He kept to one side, testing carefully with his weight as he progressed. The noise upstairs continued, a regular metallic banging coming from over the wood shop. Spraggue reviewed the plan of the theater in his head. The stage was over the shop. Heavy metallic thuds. Just the sort of noise Karen had made as she added and subtracted the bricklike counterweights from the carriage.

Spraggue doubled his pace. If someone were playing with the weights, he'd have to catch him in the act. He'd have to find out which of the heavy iron pipes looming over the stage was dangerously underbalanced. Have to find out before any of the actors worked onstage again.

Double doors to the stage straight ahead. Spraggue's hand touched the light switch, darkened the hall. He twisted the knob silently and pushed open the right-hand door.

He could see nothing at first, the blackness was so profound. The clanging continued. The briefly opened door had gone unnoticed.

Spraggue stood in the stage-left wings, fifty feet away from the counterweight system at stage right. Fifty feet of black silence crammed with cables, steps, platforms, miscellaneous noise traps. He pressed against the back wall of the stage, started moving—cautiously, silently—toward stage right, testing the path with a stockinged foot before each step. He hardly breathed.

He was twenty feet away, when it happened. His feet came to a boundary, a barrier. It felt like a pile of lights, different sizes and shapes. He couldn't stretch across it, couldn't find the inches of bare floor to stand on. If he moved against them, the lights would roll, careen into one another. The joker would flee.

Spraggue tensed. Only twenty feet away, the noise from the counterweights was still rhythmic. He lowered himself to his knees, hands scrabbling on the floor for the proper utensil. His outstretched right arm touched a C-clamp. It would have to do.

He feinted once, then tossed the C-clamp center stage. As soon as it hit, hard and loud, Spraggue turned the flash light beam full on the stage-right wings. He faced the joker.

For the first motionless seconds, Spraggue thought he must be hallucinating. A nightmare apparition stood before him. A vampire: caped, gloved, hooded in black. No face, no features, only darkness. The figure shrank from the light, as if the flash-beam were some holy relic. The shape moved. Only then did Spraggue see the startled eyes.

The figure darted for the rightmost edge of the grand drape. Spraggue went after it, clambering over platforms and steps—

Afterward, he remembered the sounds very clearly. The click that must have been the rope clamp giving way, the whine of rushing ropes, the tremendous clang as the iron suspension batten, suddenly unweighted, hit the gridiron, snapped the cable, and fell. Cold air rushed by his face; the stage floor shook beneath him. He reached up, slightly ahead, and felt the thick iron bar resting at an angle, not fifteen inches from his head.

The sudden silence was piercing. Then gray dust, untouched for almost half a century, filtered down from the fly gallery and settled over the stage like choking dirty snow.

Chapter Ten

Something wet trickled down Spraggue's forehead. As he lifted a shaking hand to explore, all the stage lights flared at once. Then Karen screamed.

"Lie still," she said quickly. "I'll call an ambulance. It won't take long—"

Spraggue scrambled to his feet. "I don't need one," he said.

She caught his wrist in a steel grip. "Lie down!" Her voice gritted through clenched teeth. "The police, then. Whatever you want. Just lie down. If you could see yourself. . . ."

Spraggue stared down at his hand. His fingers were sticky where he had touched his forehead—and in the sudden glaring light, distinctly red. He raised the hand to his nose and sniffed.

"Please lie down." Karen's voice was nurse-to-hysterical-patient firm.

"I'm not hurt, Karen."

"You look—your head!"

"The pipe missed. Something spilled—"

Karen shifted her gaze from Spraggue's bloody face to the stage. She folded her arms tightly against her chest as if warding off a sudden chill.

The staircase on stage right, part of the Westenra-house set, had saved Spraggue's life. Its ornate balustrade lay shattered, but the main platform had held. One end of the iron batten straddled it, ten feet up. On stage left, unimpeded except for rehearsal furniture, the batten had crashed to the stage floor. A pool of dark liquid spread over center stage.

"Blood." Karen shivered as she knelt by the puddle. "Where would someone get all that blood?"

Spraggue held up a battered tin bucket. "I was afraid the

company ghost was monkeying with the weights. Now it looks as if he had something less lethal on his mind."

"You could have been killed."

"By mistake. If I hadn't interrupted him—"

"Did you *see* him?" Karen asked intently.

"Not to name."

The stage manager's face fell.

"Dark eyes, I *think*. I couldn't get a fix on height with all these steps and platforms."

"Sex?"

Spraggue sighed. "A black, shapeless cloak—the same outfit that baffled Eddie yesterday. I thought he was a fool for not noticing more. I'll have to apologize."

"But even with a cape," Karen insisted, "you can tell something about shape. Can't you rule Gus Grayling out? He's fat."

"Whoever it was *moved* well, like a thin person. I couldn't hear footsteps when he ran."

"What about Emma? Can't you rule her out?"

"I'd hate to think I couldn't recognize that body anywhere."

"Close your eyes. See it again, just the way it was," Karen ordered.

"I'm *almost* sure it couldn't have been Emma," Spraggue said.

"Dark eyes," Karen muttered. "Dark eyes. Darien's are blue. That lets him out. Eddie can't see without his glasses. . . ."

"Wait a minute, Karen. I said I *thought* he had dark eyes. I'm not sure."

"What else have we got to go on?" she said angrily. "You're a trained observer, as an actor and a detective! I'm just voting to trust your first impression."

"Thanks. But as far as eliminating suspects, you're the only one absolutely in the clear."

"Me!" The stage manager's right hand came up almost automatically and Spraggue prepared to dodge the slap. It never came. Instead Karen began to laugh. "Me," she repeated incredulously.

"You all right?" Spraggue asked.

"I will be. I've got to get a crew in to clean all this up. Someone to replace the batten. . . . Darien will have three kinds of fits—"

"Let him," Spraggue said. "Help me reconstruct the trick. Then you can call Arthur."

"I'll look around," she said, "while *you're* cleaning up. You

64

look like Jack the Ripper. Towels and soap in the dressing room. Use *cold* water. Hot water just sets the stain."

"Back in two minutes. Look, theorize, but *don't touch anything.*"

Karen searched, her hands firmly clasped behind her back to avoid temptation. By the time Spraggue returned, damp but unbloodied, she had found the bits of rope—one tied around the bucket, one connected to a batten near the fallen pipe.

"The bucket must have dropped," she said. "Did you hear it?"

"No. But if it fell with the pipe, one sound would have drowned out the other."

"Okay, Spraggue. So what we have is one bucket filled with blood hanging from a batten. Ropes to two different battens. What was our vampire up to?"

"A blood bath, I think," said Spraggue. "What's rehearsing tomorrow morning?"

"Act Two."

"Can you take down the batten with the rope attached? We'll have to reconstruct the trick exactly to determine the intended victim."

"Sure." Karen moved off into the wings.

"Take it down *slowly.*"

The heavy bar descended, bare except for the crystal chandelier—and a length of rope, tied to the pipe at one end.

"All right," said Karen, striding back onstage. "Show off. Isn't this where you're supposed to take a quick look at the knot and pronounce it the work of a left-handed midget from South Carolina?"

Spraggue examined the rope, the piece tied to the batten and the piece on the bucket. Dime-store clothesline doubled up and tied with plain square knots. "Sorry to disappoint you," he said.

"So the bucket is tied to the batten . . ." she prompted.

"To the two battens," Spraggue corrected.

"Ah."

"What?"

"I see it," Karen said grimly. "What a rotten—"

"How?"

"It's easy. The batten that fell, that was the stationary support. The joker attached the bucket."

"Yes."

"But then he also attached it to another pipe, circling the rope

65

around the bucket's middle. And the pipe he attached it to is Number 6."

"So?"

"So Number 6 *moves,* Spraggue. During Act Two, scene two. I raise it about two feet."

"Why?"

"To clear the chandelier out of the way before the next scene change. One less thing to do later."

Spraggue nodded. "When Number 6 batten goes up, the bucket tips over. Who's beneath?"

"Act Two," Karen murmured. "Let me check the prompt-book."

She was gone less than a minute. Spraggue never lost the sound of her footsteps.

"Act Two." She reappeared and positioned herself onstage, lining up carefully with the fallen batten, stationing herself even with the shredded rope. "It would have been Emma."

"Emma," he echoed, seeing her bright red hair darkened with blood.

"Why Emma?"

"Why any of them?" Spraggue said sharply. "Why Georgie or Deirdre? Why Greg Hudson? Why Eddie?"

"All of them? What happened to Georgie?"

"It's not important, Karen. I'd tell you if it were."

"Both brides," Karen said. "Jonathan Harker, Renfield. . . ."

"What?" Spraggue said suddenly.

"Nothing. I'm just renaming them, the ones who were attacked. Saying their character names instead of their real names—"

"Say them again. Just the same way!"

"The brides of Dracula, Jonathan Harker, Renfield, Lucy Westenra—what is it, Michael?"

Spraggue was too deep in thought to notice that Karen Snow had finally used his first name. "The *order,* Karen. Dracula must have attacked the brides, right? Or they wouldn't be vampires. Then he gets Harker. He's the first victim in the book, while he's visiting the Count in Transylvania. Then it's off to England and Renfield. And who's the next victim?"

"Lucy," Karen answered eagerly.

"Emma," Spraggue said at the same time.

"You think the prankster is playing according to the script?" Karen said.

"I hope not."

"Why?"

"Because Lucy is the first to die."

"But if we *know* who's next, if we understand the message, then we can prevent—"

"Message," Spraggue said. "The message. You're good for me, Karen. Look around. If I'm right, there should be a scrap of paper around. . . ."

"Wait." Karen halted in midsearch. "What about Frank, Michael? You forgot Frank."

"Shit." Spraggue sank down onto a platform. "You're right. Frank was attacked and he played Dr. Seward—"

"And Seward is never attacked by Dracula," Karen finished the thought.

"Damn."

"Could be the exception that proves the rule," Karen said hopefully.

Spraggue smiled. "You're too kind."

She flashed that half-there smile at him. "I mean it. I don't think you should throw the theory out yet. It could help us prepare for the next attack."

Spraggue thought back to the script. "On Caroline," he said.

"Unless there's a repeat attempt on Emma."

"Let's find the note."

It was behind the counterweight carriage, slightly crumpled. Spraggue picked it up gingerly with the edge of a handkerchief. The surface was probably too rough to hold fingerprints anyway. He recognized the printing immediately: numbers again: III4122

"Karen," he said. "Downstairs in my dressing room. A book on the makeup table. Old brown leather. *Macbeth.* Look up Act Three, scene four, line one hundred twenty-two."

She stared at him blankly for a moment, then disappeared.

Spraggue continued to search the stage. What for, now? Some clue, any item the joker might have dropped in his hurried getaway. Something to make up for the lack of description, the failure to apprehend. Karen's footsteps clattered up the stairs. They hesitated, then crossed the stage.

"Yes?" he said, not looking up.

"Blood will have blood," she said, holding out the battered volume.

Spraggue took it and read:

"It will have blood, they say; blood will have blood.
Stones have been known to move and trees to speak;"

They stood immobile for a minute. Karen shivered.
"I think it's time to call Darien," Spraggue said.

Chapter Eleven

"Not now, Spraggue!" Darien whispered furiously the next morning. "Haven't I got enough to worry about? Repairmen all over my stage—"

"Karen can take care of that. I have to talk to you."

"Look, I talked to you damn near all night—"

"*Now,* Arthur," Spraggue said firmly.

Red-faced, the director excused himself from the bustle onstage. He dodged the scaffolding stage right and huddled with Spraggue in the wings.

"Make it brief," Darien said, softening his words with a crooked grin.

"Arthur," Spraggue said bluntly. "Why aren't you playing straight with me?"

"I don't know what you mean." Darien's blue eyes stayed cool.

"Recognize this?" Spraggue held up the copy of the note he'd found while searching Darien's office.

"Where did you—" Darien began, then stopped abruptly.

"Right." Spraggue smiled. "You blew your line. You're supposed to say 'What's that?' Then I might have believed you when you said you hardly ever look at your desk. But now it's too late for that."

"Where do you get off searching my office? Going through my personal things?"

"If you're not going to cooperate—"

"I don't have to tell you anything, Spraggue. You hear me? Anything!"

"That's right, Arthur. And I don't have to work for you. Find someone else to listen while you spin half a fairy tale—"

"I told you the truth!"

"Selections from the truth! It's not the same thing."

"If you hadn't let the bastard waltz by you last night—"

"You're right, Arthur." Sprague lowered his voice, "With the information you gave me, all I could hope for was a lucky break. I had one last night, a break that could have been very *un*lucky for me. Maybe the next time—"

"I doubt there'll *be* a next time, Sprague. For you. I don't need anyone questioning me, searching my office, treating me like a criminal! I hired you!"

"And you can fire me, Arthur. Anytime," Sprague said. He waited for the words to come. After all that uncertainty over taking the job, Sprague found himself surprised at how fiercely he longed to keep it.

"Boss?" The fat man stepped silently out of the shadows. Sprague wondered how long he'd stood there, hidden by the glaring lights and the dark enveloping curtains.

"What do you want, Dennis?" Darien said sharply.

"Nothing to get excited about. Business. Sorry. I didn't realize I was interrupting an important conference—"

"It's all right, Dennis," Darien said, his voice granting reluctant forgiveness.

"I haven't met Mr. Sprague, you know," the fat man continued. Sprague gazed at him, puzzled. He'd expected the house manager to take the rebuff, excuse himself, and melt back into the shadows. Didn't realize he was interrupting an important— Dennis Boland knew exactly what he was butting in on, unless he was deaf.

Darien performed perfunctory introductions.

"I'll talk to you about my little problem later, boss," the fat man said. "Sure hope nothing else happens to disturb your cast. They're plenty upset as it is."

"I know that, Dennis," Darien said.

"Good. I'll be getting back to work then. Come by and see me when you have a chance. Nothing urgent."

The fat man shook hands all around, effaced himself, and disappeared back into darkness. Sprague listened to his surprisingly light footsteps fade. Too soon? Had Dennis stopped to hear the end of the conversation?

Darien ran a hand through his wispy, thinning hair and sighed. "I don't have to tell you how upset I am, do I?" he said.

Sprague let out his breath. He wasn't going to be fired. The fat man's intrusion had taken the wind out of Darien's sails. A timely interruption.

70

"I still have to know why you didn't show me that note, Arthur."

Darien shrugged. "It seemed so silly at the time," he said lamely. "Anonymous notes." He wrinkled his nose in distaste.

"If I'm going to find out who the joker is, I have to know *everything* that's going on," Spraggue insisted.

"Would it have made any difference if you'd seen that note at the beginning?"

"Maybe. I would have placed the joker in a different league. I thought I was dealing with a bizarre sense of misplaced humor at the start. Now I believe he—or she—is serious. That letter might have led me there sooner. 'One suicide not enough.' Not the sort of sentiment I'd have expected from a common prankster."

"But it's so damned ridiculous!" Darien exploded. "Does whoever-it-is imagine that I'm going to cringe in terror and throw myself out some window?"

"The thing is," Spraggue said, "whoever-it-is seems to be sending someone in the company messages. Messages I'm sure at least one person understands. . . ."

"I don't follow you."

"There are messages that go with the tricks. So far all of them, except yours, have been sent in code—"

"Can you understand them?"

"I think so."

"Mine wasn't in code," Darien said. "He must have realized I wouldn't understand."

"Maybe."

"What about the others, Spraggue? What do they mean?"

"They're all warnings. And I think we have to take them seriously."

"Against anyone in particular?"

"Against almost everyone, in time," Spraggue said.

Darien raised a questioning eyebrow.

"Right now," Spraggue continued, "I'm most concerned about Emma and Caroline. Emma should have been the victim of last night's prank. The joker may not be satisfied with a botched attempt."

"Why Caroline?"

"She's after Emma."

"Can't you explain, Spraggue?"

"I'd rather not. It's only a theory. But what I want to do is to call in the police and have those two women protected at least until the opening—"

"No police."

"Arthur. . . ."

"Absolutely not. Look, I agree with you. We're dealing with someone who has to be taken seriously, with someone very disturbed. But what has he accomplished so far? That attack last night wasn't meant to harm you, that's what you said. And a bucket of blood would have upset Emma dreadfully, but it wouldn't have killed her! And my note—what harm is there in that? I'm not suicidal. Even if I were, I doubt I'd have been driven off my nut by an anonymous communication.

"I think you're getting very close now, Michael. You know where to look, who the next victim might be. You can handle this without the police, without the publicity. I'm sure of it."

"Mr. Darien." The voice was Karen Snow's. "We're ready. Do you want to go with the scene? Only thirty-five minutes to lunch break."

"A whole morning wasted!" Darien's fingernails dug into his palms. "Let's try to salvage something, Spraggue. The joker won enough last night; he's ruined a morning's rehearsal. Let's not give him any more satisfaction. No publicity. Let's just get back to work."

"It's your show, Arthur."

"Call places for Act Two, scene three, Karen. Quickly!"

Spraggue took a seat in the audience, third-row center, to wait for his cue. He nodded to Gregory Hudson, slouched comfortably four rows back, sandwiched between Deirdre and Georgina. A breathing contradiction, that tall effeminate man always surrounded by women. Were the ladylike manner, the high voice, only outward tricks of nature?

The two brides of Dracula giggled and whispered with Harker, their laughter reaching a peak when Caroline Ambrose, in a simple but expensive black dress, entered and dropped languidly into a front row seat next to Arthur Darien.

The scene began, a full technical run-through with lights, music, and sound effects. The fog machines hummed faintly. Blue mist poured out over the rocky coast of Whitby, England. Music played—plaintive lingering strings joined by a lonely clarinet. A wolf howled an eerie descant. A pleasurable chill crept up Spraggue's spine.

Emma Healey appeared stage center on the highest platform, eyes wide and vacant, unnaturally pale in the indigo light.

"Enter Lady Macbeth, mad," whispered a voice from behind.

Spraggue turned sharply: Hudson's voice. Deirdre smirked and covered her mouth with her hand. Spraggue wondered: did Hudson often quote *Macbeth*?

Emma's hair flamed around her oval face. She wore the same low-cut blue leotard with the addition of a long rehearsal skirt "to give her the feel" of the floaty nightgown she would wear in performance. She held out her arms to an invisible presence and spoke. Spraggue drew in his breath.

Her voice was deep and throaty, loud enough to be heard at the back of the house, yet somehow intimate. "You bade me come, Master," she said, pausing before the final word. Her delivery was supremely sexy—a suntan-oil commercial oozing with class. Spraggue could hear Greg Hudson's running commentary behind him, envying the luck of the vampire. Silently, Spraggue agreed.

In a rush of wind, young Lucy Westenra heard Dracula's answer, deep and melodious.

"Come closer!" the voice beckoned, tempted, as well as commanded. Spraggue searched for the actor. His voice came from everywhere, careening off the walls.

Lucy-Emma's voice was longing, yet afraid. "Nearer the edge? I dare not."

"Fear not, my child, my Lucy. I will protect you. You *will* come."

Slowly, the woman descended the twisting, rocky steps.

"No!" Darien's shout broke the mood. "Look *up*, Emma. Up! Focus on your vision of the vampire."

"I'm afraid I'll fall. I'm not used to the steps."

"Tell her Deirdre would be happy to try, Arthur," Greg Hudson volunteered. "That'll get her eyes off the floor."

"Shhhhh."

The offstage voice continued hypnotically. "Come, my Lucy, my bride. Blood of my blood, you will be. Flesh of my flesh. Years have I waited since your image first enthralled me—"

"But Arthur," Caroline Ambrose stage-whispered, "just look at her! She should be *virginal*, don't you think? Not *panting*."

"Shhhhh." This time the hiss came not from Darien but from Hudson. Caroline glared over her shoulder.

On stage: a materialization. The heavy cover of a sarcophagus shifted magically. Fog billowed from within. A black shape arose, back to the audience, cloak outstretched.

Spraggue searched for the familiar stage mechanisms, fixed

on the area below the sarcophagus, carefully screened from audience view, postulated the hydraulic lift, the trapdoor. The illusion was perfect.

Arthur Darien's voice interrupted Spraggue's concentration. "You better get ready for your entrance, Caroline," he said.

"What? And miss the sexy part?" Greg intoned to his giggling camp followers.

Spraggue watched as Caroline shot him a grim look, walked briskly up the stairs, and disappeared into the wings.

The Count, John Langford, majestic in profile, held out his arms toward Emma. Helplessly drawn to him, yet somehow repulsed, she moved unwillingly down the steps, awake but entranced. The scene was more ballet than theater. The principal dancers turned, eyed each other hungrily. Their hands met. As she neared the bottom of the staircase, the Count swept her off her feet. His hand stroked her hair, fondled her throat. She fell back in his arms, accentuating the line from long neck to swelling breast. The vampire bit. She sighed, cried out. Gently the Count draped her fainting form over the sarcophagus; carefully he loosened the high collar of her imaginary gown. With a flourish of black velvet, he leaned over her—

"Damn, she's good!" Georgina breathed from the back row. Someone grunted agreement.

Spraggue found himself caught up in the action in a way he thought he'd outgrown. They were on fire, those two. Their eyes, the way they claimed each other—some of the best theatrical moments came in silence.

The Count smoothed Emma's fiery hair. His hand slid down her cheek, lingered at her neck, caressed her breast. . . .

A terrified cry from offstage shattered the mood. Caroline Ambrose made her entrance.

"Hold it!" Darien shouted. "Give them more time, Caroline! When John puts her on the bench, give him a full five count, even an eight. Better still, forget the offstage yell. Too distracting. Come on in silence. Let us get used to seeing you up there. Lights! Get a baby spot on her as soon as she enters. Not too bright. Then look around, Caroline. Right! Remember the fog. Try to see *through* it. You *think* you see her, but you're not sure. Right. So the cry is more *tentative*. Lovely work, John and Emma. Take it from the bench."

"Think the Count needs a stand-in?" Spraggue was surprised to find Greg Hudson in the seat beside him. The brides of Dracula were gone. "They've got to get ready for the next scene,"

74

said Hudson, "in case the master decides to go right on. We have to anticipate his moods." Hudson leaned back in his seat, eyes fastened on the set. "They do work well together, don't they?"

Spraggue nodded agreement.

"Almost as if they'd been practicing a long time. Emma's a very busy little girl."

Spraggue said nothing.

"I don't see how Langford could have managed it," Hudson went on speculatively, almost to himself. "Not the way Lady Caroline smothers him with affection."

Darien interrupted the scene again. Caroline had come in too fast.

"I wonder which of them will explode first," Greg said.

"What do you mean?"

"One of the ladies is about to throw bricks. Probably Emma. She's keyed up, you know. Scared."

"About the role?"

"Are you kidding? Look at her. She'll steal this show away from Caroline Ambrose without dropping a bra strap."

"Then what's she afraid of?" Spraggue kept his voice low. He didn't want to disturb Darien, who stared so attentively, so single-mindedly at the stage.

"Nothing, I suppose," Greg said. "Some phone calls."

"Anonymous?"

"Yeah. The breather routine. Calls in the middle of the night. Usually I get the phone. Waste of the guy's efforts."

"It's a man?"

"Man, woman. I can't tell. But it gets on Emma's nerves. She's having trouble sleeping."

Is this meant to tell me that Emma confines her fornicating to you? Spraggue wondered. Warning me off? Spraggue searched Greg's intent face. His eyes never left Emma . . . or John Langford.

"Watch her!" Greg said. "Caroline. She's going to blow the scene again."

Caroline made her entrance in the grand manner, distracted. She was panting, flushed with exertion. Her devotion to Lucy was such that she had run all the way from the house to the cliffs. She posed, tragic in the fog.

"Lucy!" she shouted, her voice too loud, strident. It broke the mood. Spraggue's eyes stayed with Lucy and the Count. Their passion was inspirational.

In his chair, Darien rumbled like a volcano about to erupt.

Greg Hudson dug his elbow into Spraggue's ribs and gave a knowing nod in Darien's direction.

"Serves him right for casting the bitch," he whispered.

"Shit!" Darien controlled himself with effort, started over in his most reasonable tone. "Caroline, dear, what I am trying to do here—" Spraggue remembered that voice from the old times in England. Darien at his angriest.

The harangue was postponed by a commotion at stage left. A brawl, it sounded like. Accusatory voices rang out. The stage manager demanded silence. Something crashed to the floor. A small terrier puppy, yapping furiously, bounded onto the stage, Karen Snow in hot pursuit.

"Caroline!" Darien thundered. "What is that creature doing in the theater?"

"Arthur, it's not my fault. I put him in my dressing room. Well, I *couldn't* leave him in that hotel room all day, could I? Someone must have let him out."

The dog yipped.

"Just get him off my stage!" Darien yelled.

"I'm trying," Karen answered through clenched teeth.

Caroline began a new scene. "Did you miss me, Wolfie?" she cooed down at the frightened animal. Her eyes searched the stage. "Eddie, is that you, darling?"

"God," Hudson groaned. "Can't she leave the undergraduates alone?"

Eddie Lafferty appeared sheepishly from the wings.

"You'll help me, Eddie, won't you?" Caroline pointedly ignored Karen's efforts to trap the animal. "You can catch him. Don't panic him now," she admonished the seething stage manager. "Just leave him be until I come down and—"

"Stay where you are, Caroline! I want this scene finished! Karen, get that mutt off the set!" Darien stayed seated, but his voice indicated that he wouldn't remain so for long.

The small dog was now pursued by the stage manager, Eddie Lafferty, and a stagehand whose name Spraggue didn't know. Caroline shouted advice from above, like some divine being. "He won't bite you. He's really very friendly. Call him. His name is Wolf. Don't hurt him. Don't scare him like that!"

It was Karen who organized the successful maneuver. The three pursuers cornered the panicked animal. Eddie scooped him up and displayed him like a trophy. Everyone else applauded, except for Darien.

"Thank you, Eddie dear." Caroline ignored Karen's and the

stagehand's contribution to the rescue. She came down a few steps. "Now just put him in his basket—"

"Stop!" Eddie's voice, usually so deferential, gave the order. "Stay where you are. Freeze!" He pushed the dog into the arms of the gaping stagehand, and raced up the uneven steps, past the platform where John and Emma sat hand in hand. He knelt at the first riser.

"What the hell is going on?" Darien demanded, standing.

Caroline placed a hand eloquently over her heart and gasped. She collapsed elegantly on the fifth step of the long twisting flight.

Eddie straightened up slowly, holding something carefully in his hands. Emma and John stared at it wordlessly.

"Will someone tell me *what* is going on?" inquired Darien.

"It's a trip wire," Eddie said too loudly.

Caroline burst into beautifully orchestrated tears. With a regretful glance at Emma, John Langford took the steps two at a time to comfort her.

"A trip wire?" Darien repeated.

"A thin piece of wire strung between two nails driven into the riser."

"But—" Emma began.

"Yes?"

"But I came down those steps, Arthur. You saw me. It wasn't there."

"I picked you up before you reached the bottom step," John Langford corrected her.

"Just the way you always do, darling." Caroline's voice had turned to ice. "Emma wasn't in any danger. She knew that. She knew it when she planted the damn thing—"

Langford placed a warning hand on Caroline's shoulder. "Stop it, Caroline. You don't know what you're saying. You're upset."

"Let her talk, John. I'm fascinated," said Emma defiantly.

"How dare you, you—"

Spraggue stood up. "Arthur," he said, "clear the stage. Get all the lights on and break for lunch. Karen, there's a leather case in my dressing room. Could you send someone to get it? And could you stay?"

Darien gaped. Then he shrugged. "An hour for lunch," he said. "Be back at one-thirty. Now clear the set."

Caroline sniffed loudly. "Take me down to my dressing room, John. I'm not hungry—"

Langford escorted the weeping Caroline down the stairs, gazing helplessly at Emma. It was Caroline's best performance of the day. She gave Emma one reproachful stare, kissed Eddie gratefully on the cheek, reclaimed her puppy, and allowed Langford to half-carry her from the stage. Spraggue restrained his applause.

The theater began to empty, though some of the actors hesitated, watching Spraggue curiously as he removed a magnifying lens from the leather case a stagehand had brought up. Darien was the last to leave.

"Well," said Karen Snow, her lips tightly pressed together, "you asked me if I thought the other actors knew why you were here. They're not *that* dumb. They're on to you now."

"Good."

"Why?"

"The joker's been giving us warnings. I wanted to return the favor."

"So he's warned," she said. "What next?"

"Either he gets more careful, he stops, or he gets caught," Spraggue said.

"I hope he stops," Karen said.

"Not me. I'm starting to look forward to meeting this joker of ours. I hope the bastard doesn't quit."

"Just make sure you catch him soon."

Chapter Twelve

There were fingerprints on the riser—too many. Eddie's, of course, and probably the prints of the stagehand who'd set up the platforms and the carpenter who'd built them. Spragague photographed them all, feeling vaguely silly. Now he'd have to fingerprint the entire cast. And he was certain the joker had used gloves. Everyone used gloves. He inspected the nails, driven in clean and straight. Could tiny Georgina swing the necessary blow? The wire itself, Karen identified easily; right off a roll in the electrician's booth. Kept on an open shelf in an unlocked room. Available to all.

Spragague shook his head, disgusted. "You'd better go get some lunch while there's still time," he said to Karen.

"What about you?"

"Not hungry."

"Did the joker leave you another note?"

"Can't find one."

"I'll bring you back a sandwich," she said.

Spragague went to pay a condolence call on Caroline Ambrose. Her dressing-room door was partially open.

Caroline was alone, standing in front of her full-length mirror. She preened, testing one famous expression after another. Her smile faded and her fingers gently massaged her temples, her forehead, desperately smoothing age-wrinkled skin.

The face reflected in the glass was a classic. Caroline Ambrose had huge violet eyes under arching brows, porcelain skin, delicate bones, a cloud of dark hair, and a sweet triangular smile. Cloying, Spragague corrected himself, not sweet. A self-conscious smile designed to evade laugh lines. Appraising eyes that constantly searched, for approval, for weakness, for gain.

Caroline mascaraed her long lashes, replenished her scarlet lipstick, patted more color into her cheeks. She made Spraggue long for the uncompromising face of Karen Snow, not beautiful, but real. He much preferred the intelligence in Karen's eyes to the fake docility in Caroline's.

Spraggue rapped at the open door. Caroline was still engrossed in her reflection.

She turned, offered him a three-quarter profile and a madonna smile. It was one of her best. She was often photographed that way.

"May I come in, Miss Ambrose?" Spraggue said with what he hoped was the right touch of deference for a request from a second lead to a star.

Her triangular smile widened speculatively. She patted a place on the bench close beside her and beamed as he sat down.

"Call me Caroline, Michael. Please."

"Caroline." He said her name lightly, approvingly. "I hope my knock didn't frighten you."

"Oh, no."

"Good. After what you've been through—"

"Just frightful, isn't it?" She shivered, then smiled at her pretense. "The things actors have to put up with."

"You, especially."

Caroline flushed with pleasure. "So you, at least, have noticed. There is such envy in the theater."

"You seem to take it very calmly. If you had gone a few more steps down that staircase—"

She put a hand on his arm. "Please, don't even say that. I'm not calm, not at all." She allowed a lip to quiver. "Really, I shouldn't have been left here alone."

So John Langford had deserted her. For Emma? "I'm sorry," Spraggue said.

"I'm being foolish, I know." Caroline smiled bravely. "But I can't dwell on such things. It might affect my performance."

It certainly wasn't affecting her performance at the moment, Spraggue thought.

"These things have happened to me before, you know."

"Trip wires?"

"No, no. But my dressing room has been broken into twice— and I have had setbacks in my career. Jealous people who've taken advantage—"

"Do you know who set that wire?"

80

"Why, no, Michael. I *feel* it. I'm very sensitive to these things. I feel who my enemies are. I always have enemies."

"Have you discussed your suspicions with Darien?"

"Arthur? He never listens to me. He believes in the goodness of humanity at large, particularly the female gender. It's one of the truly delightful things about him."

"You've known him a long time."

"We do go back a ways. But then," she smiled archly, "I understand you know Arthur from your past as well."

Terrific. Just what he needed: a discussion of his own past. Lesson number two: get the man to talk about himself. Even without a script, Caroline sounded programmed. He said nothing. Let her think he was hard of hearing.

After a moment's pause, she chattered on. "Arthur and I have been friends forever, really. I am so grateful to him. It's the old story: he took me under his wing from my first New York show, and we've never really lost touch. I depend on him so much. He and Spider and I were the three musketeers for a while. You could never find one of us without the other two."

"Spider?"

"Dennis, Dennis Boland. I shouldn't call him Spider. He hates it, really. An old childhood nickname. Sometimes they can be so hard to lose."

Spragerue murmured agreement.

"Haven't you met him? A dear man. He's the house manager here. So devoted to Arthur—and to me."

With a start Spragerue realized that it was his line, that he was expected to say something like "That shouldn't be too difficult," to take part in the flirtatious little skit Caroline Ambrose was constructing.

He picked up his cue, somewhat tardily. Caroline beamed. He had passed the test. From now on, he would be Michael Spragerue, that charming young actor. He bit his lip.

"It's rather a sad tale," she rattled on. "Spider—Dennis—comes from a very cruel background, very poor. He and Arthur were boyhood friends in New York. They lost touch. It's so easy to lose touch. Arthur always had that genius, you know. Scholarships, Eastern colleges. And then when he was a successful New York director, he went to a party. And there was Spider, his best friend from the hard times. I don't think they've been separated since." She sighed deeply. Every word had been spoken as if rehearsed many times before, each gesture, every

81

graceful turn of the head choreographed. The sigh completed the tale. It was again his cue. Spraggue searched for the expected line.

"And you became Spider's friend, too."

She opened her violet eyes wide. "But of course. He is a darling man. I was married to Domingo, my third husband, then. Domingo de Renza."

She paused. Spraggue nodded encouragement. De Renza, huh? Emma hadn't exaggerated about the wealth of Caroline's ex.

"Domingo took a great liking to Spider." Caroline laughed, a carefully calibrated trill. "He visited us at the plantation, almost lived with us." With a graceful arm movement, she indicated a lush mass of spotted and streaked violet and yellow blooms. "Domingo still sends me flowers, you know. Every day. And Spider arranges them for me. He adores orchids, and he knows how much it pleases me to have them done really well."

"How kind of him," Spraggue said, feeling that he'd become enmeshed in a drawing-room comedy, seeking vainly to return to the question of who she thought had arranged the trip wire. Not that her opinion would hold much water. She lived in fantasyland.

"I love coming down to the dressing room each morning to find something delicate and exotic. Domingo understood that part of me so well." She detached one violet spray from the arrangement and held it against her cheek. "I rarely wear them, but just knowing they're available picks up my spirits. That's why I think she took them that day."

"She?"

"*Emma*, darling. That *is* what we're talking about, isn't it? Who set up the trip wire. Perhaps I shall wear some of my orchids to Arthur's party."

"When did Emma take your flowers?"

"Let me see. Not long ago. Last Monday, I think it was. Naturally, she denied it. But I knew. I always know. She wants everything I have. She already has that lovely role and now—" Caroline caught herself. She had been frowning. She checked her image in the mirror to make sure no wrinkles remained. "Arthur must have told you about his party. Tomorrow night. Right here in the theater—"

"What about dress rehearsal?"

"Check your schedule, darling. The technical people will be doing some dreary run-through onstage, but the front-of-the-house areas will be devoted to the party. Black tie, just like the galas old what's-his-name, that man who killed himself here—"

"Phelps."

"That's it. Arthur's so keen on the idea. Just like old Phelps used to throw. All the actors, members of the press, plenty of photographers. . . ."

Darien had mentioned it. The chance to meet the backers of the show.

"I suppose you already know most of the people really involved in producing the show. As the star—"

Nothing he might have said could make her happier. Her eyes lit up.

"Well, I do know some of the more influential backers—"

"Any of them coming up from New York? Or is Arthur keeping this a local venture?"

"Why, darling"—she batted her eyelashes—"I really couldn't say. Jamie Blakeley *could* be considered local. He has *pieds à terre* in so many cities. He practically *insisted* on my being in the show. He's the one who gave me my little dog."

Spraggue filed the name away. Blakeley. Aunt Mary would know him and he would know the other backers. Caroline chattered on, leaving him no chance for escape.

A huge party at the theater. Actors, director, press. Terrific. What an opportunity for the joker.

Spraggue heard wary footsteps behind him. Caroline halted in midsentence and gushed: "Oh, Dennis, darling, I was just telling Michael all about you and how much you do for the company and here you come right on cue. Michael Spraggue, meet Dennis Boland."

The fat man smiled, but the smile wasn't pleasant. "We've met," he said. Spraggue was forcibly reminded of the despised childhood name, Spider. The house manager looked like a great bloated spider hanging in the corner of the room.

"How nice," Caroline said blankly. "Mr. Spraggue's been asking me absolutely penetrating questions about the company ghost. I think he's been hiding his true vocation from us."

Neither of the men responded.

"And you did my flowers so exquisitely this morning, Dennis. It's too sweet of you."

The fat man oiled his way over to Caroline's dressing table and took her hand in his. With surprising grace, he bent and kissed it.

"It's nothing, Caroline, nothing in the world," he murmured.

Spraggue sat up straighter. He had heard that voice before. In the wings that morning, yes. But somewhere else. . . .

Caroline smiled graciously. The performance would have been perfect, except for the tiny red mark that remained on her wrist when Spider let her hand slip away.

Spraggue stood. "I'll leave you two," he said. "It's a busy day for me."

"I'm sure it is," Boland said.

Spraggue left them there, a frozen tableau, and walked down the hallway, lost in the memory of an unctuous voice. Then he had it. One line: "I just hope you know what you're doing," spoken behind Darien's closed office door.

Chapter Thirteen

"Psssst!"

Spraggue stopped in his tracks. The conspiratorial hiss came from his left, somewhere up ahead, off the passageway. It was repeated, louder. A handle turned and a doorway pushed open an inch. Dracula himself motioned Spraggue inside his dressing room and swiftly closed the door.

John Langford was a good two inches taller than Spraggue's six feet one. He dressed with a contrived casualness that must have cost. Designer jeans, leather vests, elegantly tailored shirts that clung to his broad shoulders and fashionably tapered torso. A thin gold chain around his neck. The intensity he gave to every performance was visible now. It kept him from looking ridiculous as he raised a warning finger to his lips and jerked open the connecting door. No eavesdroppers.

Spraggue felt as if he'd been dragged into some den from the Arabian Nights. Caroline Ambrose had restricted her dressing-room decor to orchids and some twenty photos of herself in various roles, including an unmistakable Lady Macbeth. Langford's dressing room had been completely transformed.

It had a rug. None of the others did. A worn but garish Oriental too large for the space, it rolled at one end. Spraggue decided that it must have been confiscated from the properties department. All chairs but one had been removed and replaced by piles of bright orange and purple cushions. The single ornate chair was the mate to Darien's office throne. What gave the place such a cavernous air was its lack of light. Heavy dark cloth had been tacked over the two high windows. Candles in ornate brass holders flickered.

"I cannot allow the sunlight," said Langford tersely. "I told Arthur we should rehearse only by night, but he would not

85

accommodate me. Often, when the sun is too bright, when I feel I cannot stand the glare, I sleep here, on my cushions, until such time as the vampire can safely walk."

Spraggue nodded, grateful that no other response seemed expected. The late-afternoon sun hadn't seemed to bother the vampire when he'd run off with Emma in his chauffeured car. Spraggue felt the hypnotic power of Langford's presence and voice. The tone was full and deep, with faint traces of English upbringing, controlled by years of American acting. The result was diction that made everyone else on stage sound like they were reciting through mouthfuls of Cream of Wheat. The voice, a stage whisper, filled the room. What made it so special, Spraggue decided, was its enormous *power*. At absolute full volume, Langford always seemed to have a lion's roar still in reserve.

The actor sank cross-legged to the carpet, spread his palms on his knees, nodded at Spraggue to join him. When their eyes were on a level, Langford spoke:

"I do think Arthur might have consulted me before bringing in a detective."

Spraggue grinned. His identity was no secret anymore.

"He's overreacting, of course," Langford continued. "No real harm done yet. If Arthur had just asked me—"

"I'm sure Arthur didn't want to distract you from your performance," Spraggue said. A little flattery seemed called for.

Langford beamed.

"I'd be very glad to hear any ideas you might have about the joker." Keep it humble.

Langford's face turned solemn. "I take the psychological approach myself," he said condescendingly.

"Ah." Spraggue nodded, young Hawkshaw to veteran sleuth. All he had to do for this investigation was to figure out which part he'd been cast for in each actor's fantasy. Caroline wanted flirtatiousness; Langford wanted respect, recognition of his authority. Spraggue found himself wholeheartedly sharing Karen's antipathy for members of the second oldest profession. Difficult, since he had to count himself among the membership.

"Take a man like Gus Grayling," Langford said sagely.

"I haven't met him yet."

"No need. I'll show him to you. Gus is the perfect second banana. All his life he's done the stooge parts. No heroes. No romantics. No leads. So naturally, those are the only parts he wants to play. He tries to create romance for himself. He has a tortuous theory about Van Helsing's frustrated passion for Mina. Don't mention it to him; he'll talk about it for days! What does a man like that want most, Spraggue?" Langford hesitated, but not long enough for an answer. He was doing a soliloquy, not a dialogue. "Attention!" Langford boomed. "And what might a man do to get attention?" He nodded slowly at Spraggue. It was time for the bright pupil to answer.

"Tricks?" suggested Spraggue.

Langford smiled. "If it weren't for one thing, I'd say that Grayling had the perfect psychological makeup for our joker. But that one thing is very powerful. Georgina!"

"Georgina? She's after Arthur Darien."

Langford closed his dark eyes, gave a careless half-smile. "They *all* love Arthur. He's a teddy bear. But he's not interested in a real woman. His mistress is this theater, this play. Gus wants Georgina. And he will get her. And that will satisfy his urge to hurt me, because, you see, I have been carefully leading him to the conclusion that *I* am interested in our young ingénue."

That would suit Langford perfectly. A faked interest in Georgina would throw Caroline off the true target of the leading man's straying affections. But would a game that fooled Gus and Caroline necessarily fool Greg Hudson? He was certainly an interested party.

Spraggue said as much to Langford.

"Hudson? A trivial personality. He must have known from the beginning that Emma cared nothing for him. Such an uneven match. A 'fling' on her part. Probably curiosity. Perhaps she felt she could 'cure' him." Langford shook his head. "I find it hard to understand bisexuals. I see Hudson as an enigma. Perhaps we'd better leave him in our field of suspects."

Perhaps we'd better! "What about Eddie?" said Spraggue.

"Shouldn't you be taking notes or something?" said Langford coolly. "I doubt I'll have time to go over this material again."

"I have an excellent memory," said Spraggue solemnly. The incredible vanity of the man!

"You suspect a man, don't you, Spraggue?"

"I haven't narrowed my suspicions down to one gender. Why do you say that?"

"You ask about the men first."

Spraggue wondered if that was a sample of Langford's psychological insight. "What do you know about Eddie Lafferty?"

"Little, I'm ashamed to say. He's hard to know. A loner. I

have noticed some attraction to our lovely stage manager—"

Damn, thought Spraggue.

"It's difficult to evaluate Lafferty because he pretends he's mad. One of these Method actors, works his role even when he's offstage. Hiding his real personality. Since he revels so in being mad, I would suppose him to be very sane, very timid, conventional. Not a very interesting subject."

"You'd prefer to go on to the women?"

"Always, my boy. Always. I won't bother to mention Emma. The idea's ridiculous! She is not a woman denied attention. But I'd have to agree with her that Caroline bears watching. I saw you come out of her dressing room. Very perceptive of you. Of course it could be something else, have nothing to do with the joker. But she is a jealous woman. Jealous and possessive. I would put her high on the list, yes, high on the list. . . . The other females. Deirdre. So intense. I dislike *intense* women. A little spooky, that one. A loner, too. Can't help you much with her. And Georgina. She's definitely out of it. A sweet idiotic child. The perfect ingénue."

"And perfect ingénues don't go around maiming dolls and setting trip wires," Spraggue finished. "Have you any thoughts on our peripheral characters—Darien, the house manager, the stage manager?"

"Foolish to include Arthur in that group. Arthur wants one thing above all, to see this show succeed. Nothing would make him jeopardize that. The others, I don't know. Technicians bore me. I find that I get along so much better with artists, with creative minds. I'm sure you understand."

Spraggue decided not to say that he understood why Karen had ranked Langford chief among the bores. Instead he tried: "Have you ever played Macbeth?"

"Often. Both Macbeth and Macduff. I've directed the play at many universities, discussed my interpretation in educational films—" The great British actor stopped suddenly. "Has this anything to do with the joker?"

"Not really," Spraggue lied. "I just find your voice so well suited to Macbeth."

"Thank you, my boy. Others join you in that opinion. Quite a few others, some very influential men of the theater."

Spraggue smiled. "And may I ask where you were Saturday night between ten and eleven o'clock?"

Langford's eyes widened. "An alibi. For me? Of course we haven't discussed me. But from a psychological point of view, I assure you, you're wasting time. I have no need for more glory than I already have. I am undisputed star of this show. I feel that my performance will greatly enhance my reputation. I have no desire to hurt my fellow actors in any way. And I am quite satisfied with my personal life."

No. Langford wouldn't be the joker. But with that colossal ego, that incredible vanity, he might well be the target.

"If you insist on knowing my whereabouts," Langford continued smugly, "speak to Emma. She will vouch for me— and I for her." In one fluid motion, Langford got to his feet. He crossed silently to the far wall and tapped on it three times. After a moment came the reply, three muffled raps.

"Would you be so kind as to help me out, Spraggue?" Langford smiled photogenically. His eyes glinted in the candle-light. "Just check to see that the coast is clear. I have no desire to play out one of those tedious scenes with Caroline Ambrose."

So. The next room over, the one not conveniently linked by connecting door, was the gorgeous Emma Healey's lair. And probably that was the reason for all the intrigue and secrecy. More than a need for Langford to spill his "psychological" gleanings, a need for a sympathetic goon to case the hallway and warn of Lady Caroline's approach. And Langford must have figured that anyone leaving Caroline's room after a prolonged chat would be sympathetic.

He played along, elaborately eying the hall, motioning Langford to hurry. Not until Emma's door closed did he let his face relax into a rueful grin.

How, he wondered, would Greg Hudson react to Emma's defection? A seemingly sensible guy, but one never knew. Had he realized from the beginning that Emma was not one to love exclusively? And Caroline? Did she have a script for spurned lovers? Or had she already written one for her glorious sixth marriage, to the great actor, John Langford? Would she satisfy herself with the "undergraduate" Eddie? If so, how would Karen take it? And with Karen involved, he realized abruptly, so was he.

Did all these tangled love affairs have anything to do with the joker?

Rehearsal time again. He strode hurriedly down the corridor.

Will Shakespeare had it right, he thought: "Lord, what fools these mortals be!"

Chapter Fourteen

A fifteen-minute break the next morning found Spraggue back in the Huntington Avenue phone booth. Someone had added fresh graffiti with a runny can of orange spray paint, but the phone still worked.

Aunt Mary answered on the second ring.

"Find out anything from Jamie Blakeley?" he asked.

"You again?"

"Sorry," Spraggue said hastily. "I know I'm supposed to say hello and how are you and all that, but I just haven't got the time."

"I knew I'd raised you better than—"

"Come on, Aunt Mary."

"Darling, I haven't gotten a thing from him yet. I'm meeting him for lunch at the Café Plaza. He's just the type to fall for Caroline Ambrose—"

"He wouldn't cough up the information over the phone?"

"Not a word, but don't worry. A bottle of claret with lunch and Blakeley will tell me more than I ever wanted to know about Arthur Darien's financial setup. I only hope I can keep him from telling me about his divorce again."

"You are a great lady."

"I know. And I do happen to have some fascinating information about your actors."

"Yeah?"

"Such as: Deirdre Marten is really Dinah Martowski."

"You get that from Equity?"

"No. They're remarkably closemouthed. One of the theater companies she worked for in Canada."

"Aunt Mary, would you call Fred Hurley at Police Records and give him Deirdre's real name?"

"Fred? You've got him working on this, too?"

"Yeah. And tell him he'd better hurry up."

"I refuse to browbeat him. Now listen. Does it interest you to know that your Greg Hudson is an expert in stage fighting? Taught a course in it at Carnegie-Mellon and choreographs fights when he can't get work acting."

"Intriguing avocation."

"So if he takes a swing at you, duck."

"Anything else?"

"Lots of things. Your young Renfield, for instance. He neglected to put several major credits on his résumé. He's actually done a New York Hamlet! Shakespeare-in-the-Park."

"Eddie Lafferty?"

"So his agent says."

"New York agent?"

"Right. Vacationing in Paris. My phone bill may bankrupt you."

"Did Lafferty happen to play Macbeth, too?"

"No. Why?"

"That's what I want to start focusing on. Find me any connection to *Macbeth*."

"I trust you have a reason. *Macbeth* is a fairly popular play."

"*Macbeth* was Samuel Phelps's last production in the Fens Theater. And our joker sends messages from *Macbeth*."

"Phelps," said Mary thoughtfully. "I tried to trace the family. Find out if they still had any interest in the Fens."

"And?"

"Hard going. The wife died soon after Samuel. Two sons: George and Thomas. George attempted to make a go of the theater, but failed. He tried to sell it, wound up practically giving it to Boston State. They wanted it for a school. Then their enrollment dropped and it went back on the market. It belongs to some holding company now. You know, Michael, Acme or Bonded or Universal something-or-other. I'm trying to check the title now."

"Keep after it. What about Phelps's grandchildren?"

"A blank."

"How about the résumé photos I asked for?"

"Time, Michael. It takes time. Maybe tomorrow—"

"I've got to run. Look, if I invite you to Darien's backers' gala tonight, will you come?"

"What's tonight?"

"Monday."

"Odd night for a party."

"You're telling me. Monday's 'dark night' in Boston. All the theaters are closed. That's probably why old Phelps held his soirees on Mondays. If Phelps did it, Darien can do it."

"I'd be delighted to come."

"Jamie Blakeley will be there," Spraggue warned.

"Ah. But so will John Langford." Aunt Mary sighed deeply.

"I've got to get back to rehearsal."

"Michael, I've got papers that need your signature."

"Financial drivel?"

"What else?"

"How about forgery?" Spraggue said. "I should just give you power of attorney."

"Nonsense. That's what the old and feeble give the young, not the other way around."

"I'll sign whatever you want, as soon as I get a minute."

"There's a report from your California vineyard. Not a half-bad investment."

"Praise from the master is praise—"

"Even though I suspect you went into it more for the sake of a lady than a dollar. There *is* a letter from your co-owner, Kate."

"Don't open it. It's probably obscene."

"Michael!"

"'Bye, Aunt Mary. See you tonight." He hung up and headed back toward the theater.

Had he forgotten anything? The *Macbeth* connection: Caroline had played Lady Macbeth. Langford had played Macbeth. The photos: one of the lesser-known actors could be using someone else's résumé, substituting his own photograph. Stage names . . . Hudson, an expert in stage fighting . . . Jamie Blakeley: Mary would take care of him. She'd turn him nicely inside out, inspect the stuffing, and return him to his original shape.

Spraggue took the long cool corridor to the steps, descended to the dressing rooms. Just time to scan Karen's book on Boston theater, check the index for references to Phelps, senior or junior.

Two sons: George and Thomas. Children when father Samuel had taken his life? Georgie and Tommy. No. Spraggue remembered the photograph, the white-haired gentleman with the massive beard. Must have been in his sixties when he died. Grown-up children. *What was there about that photograph?* Samuel Borgmann Phelps. Georgie Phelps. Tommy Phelps.

Georgie Phelps. *Georgina* Phelps. *Georgina Phillips!*

Spraggue found Karen's book wedged into a crack on the shelf over his makeup table. He thumbed through it as he strode down the hall toward Georgina's dressing room. Her door was closed.

Spraggue knocked. No answer. He opened the door.

The photograph was there in plain sight. Slightly younger, the beard trimmer, darker, the beady eyes unmistakable: Samuel Borgmann Phelps.

Spraggue shook his head in disbelief.

Chapter Fifteen

"Places! Three-five. Last act, last scene!" Karen's cry reverberated through the corridor, but still Spraggue didn't move.

"Spraggue? You all right?"

"Yeah."

"Anything I can do?"

"You could call me Michael."

He was rewarded with a fleeting, quickly controlled smile.

"Seriously," he said, turning away from the photo on Georgina's dressing room wall, "where's Georgie?"

"She's only on in Act One. Probably gone for a walk. Sure you're all right?"

"Fine."

"Places, then. Darien's turning blue."

Spraggue followed the stage manager up the steps.

Arthur Darien was fuming. "Where's Langford?" he demanded. "Isn't John down there? You said he was in the building—"

"In his dressing room, Arthur," Karen said soothingly. "On his way."

Caroline Ambrose, seated in the front row of the auditorium, tossed her dark hair and snorted. She crossed her legs and angrily tugged the hem of her skirt over her knees. "Does he have his little playmate with him, Karen? I *do* hope you knocked first. So embarrassing for you."

Greg Hudson, waiting in the wings for his entrance, turned and walked away. Spraggue could barely see the left side of his face, the tic jumping in his clenched jaw.

Karen ignored Caroline, taking no notice of the actress's rising voice, flushed cheeks. Darien reacted.

"Caroline," he said severely. "I don't want to see any of this onstage. You and Lucy are best friends. I don't give a damn about your sex lives and I will not have this show affected by them. Understood?"

"I'm a professional, Arthur," she answered coldly. "I do my job."

Darien squeezed her arm, gave her his best kind-uncle smile. A pudgy, heavily jowled man, lounging against the stage, giggled. Spragque stared: Gustave Grayling, easily identifiable from his résumé photo. Was Grayling chortling at the idea of Langford in trouble with both director and leading lady? Or did his jealousy of Langford exist only in that amazingly vain actor's mind?

Footsteps pounded up the stairs, raced down the hall. The missing actor appeared, out of breath, disgruntled and alone. If Emma had been with him, she'd remained below.

"Places!" Karen called, relieved.

"Arthur!" Langford approached the director. "Look, can't you do the damned ending without me? I have absolutely no desire to suffocate in that damp cramped box any longer than necessary."

"John—"

"I'm quite serious, Arthur. I abhor lying in my coffin for twenty eternal minutes only to be stabbed without uttering a single word."

"You *can't* speak in the scene, John. It's still daylight."

"And"—Langford pretended not to hear the interruption—"I despise the knife. A vampire should be staked, a wooden stake through the heart. Even a child knows that the only way to kill a vampire—"

"In the book, John," Arthur said slowly, "Dracula is killed with a Bowie knife."

"Oh, the book, the book! It's not the Bible, is it? In the *book,* as I recall, Dracula is killed by a character the playwright has not even chosen to include in this adaptation! So much for the book!"

Darien closed his eyes, spoke with effort. "In the theater, John, it is bad form to repeat the same effect twice. Understand? The first time the audience is entranced; the second time they look for the strings. We've already killed Lucy by the stake. You have to die by the knife."

Spragque waited impatiently in the stage-right wings. Karen paced.

"I think our great British actor suffers from secret claustrophobia," she said. "The way he rants about that coffin!"

"He's not going to get much sympathy from this crowd," said Spragge. "How does he die?"

"Your standard collapsing-knife trick. Gallons of chicken blood. A fatal scream. Dematerialization. Wouldn't be a bad effect if John would deign to rehearse it."

"Let's go!" shouted Darien, turning away from the still-speaking Langford.

"Places!" Karen called wearily, eyebrows imploring heaven. "Three-five. Places!"

The first half of the scene went rapidly, playing much stronger than usual. Spragge attributed the change to a new alliance, a warmth between Lady Caroline and Greg Hudson; the bond of rejected lovers.

Things bogged down at the fight.

"Stop," Darien called sadly. "Walk through it! Slow motion! Anything! I have to *see* what's screwing it up!"

Greg Hudson gritted his teeth. He knew, Spragge knew, Grayling knew: Caroline Ambrose was the disaster. She insisted on attacking the vampire killers in the "Victorian Womanly" manner, beating her fists ineffectually against Hudson's chest. Time after time, Hudson, the fight expert, ran them through the scene, trying to make Caroline less laughable. Spragge marveled at his patience.

Caroline was better at throwing fits, thank God. She shrieked convincingly as Van Helsing and Harker carried her writhing body downstage, away from the vampire's lair. But she always blew the slap.

Spragge got to hit Caroline. Director of an asylum, his character knew how to deal with hysteria. He drew back his hand, swung it around quick and hard. Caroline jerked her head away. The blow missed her chin.

"Caroline," Hudson wailed. "No! No! You have to *take* it! *Turn* with the slap. It won't hurt! He'll get you right below the cheekbone. Good sound. No danger. If you flinch like that, he could dislocate your jaw!"

"I'm sorry, Greg." Caroline fluttered her violet eyelashes. "I just got so scared!"

"It can't hurt if you're ready for it. Watch." Hudson turned to Spragge. "Hit me. Just like you tried to hit Caroline." The report was terrific. "See? Believe me, no pain. Now try it with Caroline, Spragge. Slow motion first."

At half-speed she was fine. When the blow hit her cheek, she turned with it.

"Perfect!" said Hudson warmly. "You have to *feel* it coming. The responsibility for a great slap is on the receiver, not the sender. Stand up to it, Caroline! Take it! Trust him. Spraggue won't hurt you, unless you do something unexpected."

Caroline smiled up at Spraggue tremulously.

"Take it again," ordered Hudson.

Spraggue hit out. Caroline didn't move, didn't flinch, didn't even try to turn with the slap. The force of the blow knocked her head to one side. An angry red spot flared on her cheek. She stared defiantly at Hudson.

"Good sound!" yelled Darien from below. "Keep going!"

Hudson shook his head grimly. Caroline went back to her position. She never lifted a hand to rub her stinging cheek.

Spraggue felt used, half angry at himself for hurting her, half longing to sock her again. So maybe she'd done something that deserved punishment. Maybe she was some kind of masochist. She damn well couldn't count on him to hold the whip.

He played out the rest of the scene in a trance, barely surfacing to wonder why the collapsible knife seemed so familiar. But it only tickled at his subconscious.

Chapter Sixteen

At lunch break he wangled Georgina's address and phone number out of Karen: a cheap Combat Zone hotel. Call her? No. If she were home, he'd prefer ad lib dialogue. He was getting fed up with rehearsed responses.

He stuck Karen's book on Boston theater under his arm, flagged a passing cab on Mass Ave.

Room 541. The sweating man at the desk gave him a leer. I know what you came for, brother, he seemed to say.

"Should I phone," the clerk said with a gap-toothed smirk, "or is the lady expecting you?"

"She's expecting me," Spraggue said.

The clerk made a scribbled note on a blotter. Probably kept track of visitors. In this hotel, they'd be likely to change hourly. Maybe there was a surcharge for each one.

Spraggue headed across discolored carpet to the stairs. Each flight was narrower than the last. And smelled worse. He took a deep breath on the fourth-floor landing and held it until he reached room 541.

She answered his knock quickly, with a frightened "Who's there?"

"Michael Spraggue."

"Oh. Uh. Just a minute."

She smiled as she opened the door, then stepped quickly out into the hall, pulling the door shut behind her.

"I didn't miss a scene, did I?" she asked nervously, retying the sash on her light blue robe.

"No. May I come in?"

Panic flickered briefly in her gray eyes. "Why don't you take me out for a drink, instead." The flirty offer was well-delivered, but her eyes gave her away. Was she dumb enough to keep the joker costume in plain view?

"I'd rather see your room," Sprague said. "You can show me where you found that doll."

"They don't like us to have men in the—"

"Here, Georgie? Come off it."

"I left my key inside. I'm locked out."

Sprague fiddled in his wallet for a credit card. "You're in luck. I'm a specialist in such things. I'll break in."

"No."

"I suppose they have a master key downstairs, if you'd rather."

She pulled a key from a pocket of her robe. "I guess you'd better come in," she said reluctantly.

Georgina's tiny refuge was dark. Heavy curtains shaded the window on the left. The opposite wall had a window too, so grimy that little light eked its way in. The room overlooked a bare brick wall scarcely a foot away.

"What do you want?" The smile was still there, now stubbornly set. She made no move to turn on the light.

Sprague reached for the switch. She tried to stop him, grabbed his hand. The one naked bulb glared.

His sudden intake of breath was quiet, but in the still room it echoed.

Georgina's cell was a museum, crammed with the memorabilia of life, several lives, in the theater. Aged, lacy fans framed the puny mirror: Renaissance fans, Victorian ladies' fans, burlesque queens' fans. Posters, programs, ticket stubs turned the walls into vast collages. The meager furnishings were piled haphazardly in a corner, all replaced with trunks, the proverbial theatrical trunks, plastered with destination stickers.

One trunk had the unmistakable look of a shrine. An old red shawl was draped across it, anchored by photographs. On either side of the pictures, long tapering white candles in antique brass holders.

The largest photo, the one carefully placed at the center, was a copy of the one on the dressing-room wall: Mr. Samuel Borgmann Phelps.

Wordlessly, Sprague handed Georgina the book he'd brought along, opened to the picture of the long-dead director. She studied the page, closed the volume carefully, and sat on the edge of the iron cot the hotel called a bed.

"You didn't want anyone else to succeed there," Spraggue said softly. "Samuel Phelps lost his money and his life in the Fens Theater. His son George followed in his footsteps. Is your father still alive?"

She shook her head.

"Your mother?"

She turned toward the shrine; her eyes fastened on a picture of a frail blond woman, no older than Georgina was now—a woman in costume, all in white, flowers in her hair. Ophelia?

Georgina shook her head again.

Spraggue continued: "So all you had was the theater—Phelps's dream and Phelps's folly. All but abandoned."

"The theater was a school," Georgina whispered. Spraggue had to lean close to hear her. Her lips barely moved.

"That's right," he said encouragingly.

"They were going to name it for my grandfather—"

"But instead they sold it," Spraggue said roughly. "And Arthur Darien decided to direct in your theater."

"Yes."

"And you resented it."

"No."

"And you wanted him out of your theater."

"No!"

"You want everyone out of your theater. Leave it for Samuel's ghost, for your father's ghost. So you started playing tricks."

"I didn't."

"And the *Macbeth* messages. Phelps's last play was *Macbeth*. You knew that. You even gave me a hint. Maybe you wanted to get caught. Before you really hurt someone."

"This is insane, Michael. Look at me!"

Spraggue sat on the cot next to her. He sighed. "When I look at you, I don't believe it. I can't see you lugging a bucket of sow's blood through the theater—"

"Sow's blood?"

"The stuff that was supposed to fall on Emma. I had it analyzed. Another *Macbeth* reference. Remember? One of the ingredients in the Act Four stew? 'Pour in sow's blood, that hath eaten her nine farrow. . . .'"

Georgina made a face.

"I can't see you in that black vampire suit," Spraggue said. "Too small."

"Heels," she suggested bitterly.

"I suppose. But there was no noise, no clatter—"

She let out her breath. "Then there *is* some evidence in my favor? You don't believe I'm the joker?"

"You tell me, Georgina."

She stood facing the brick wall, staring out the eyeless window. "I am Phelps's granddaughter. My name is Georgina Phelps. I took Gina Phillips as my stage name."

"Why?"

"For luck. Phelps hasn't been too lucky in the theater." She tried to laugh. "I'm not the joker, Michael. You've got to believe me."

"But the coincidence!" Spraggue began.

"Damn coincidence. There was no coincidence! I *auditioned* for this company. I want to act. And I *have* to work in the Fens Theater. Just once. To prove I can. To prove it won't get me the way it got my father and grandfather. One successful run in the Fens and I'll feel the curse is broken—"

"You seem to have brought it along with you," Spraggue said flatly.

"I don't believe in the supernatural."

"Neither do I."

"I was one of the first people attacked by the joker."

"I doubt our joker has been foolish enough to neglect to play a trick or two on himself, Georgina."

She ran both hands through her pale hair. "What can I do to make you believe me? Watch me every minute! Isolate me!"

"That'll be up to Darien."

"You can't tell him, Michael!" The color left her face so completely, Spraggue thought she would faint.

"I have to."

"He'll fire me. Michael, I'm a bit part. I don't matter to him. He won't care if I'm guilty or not. I'm bad luck; I'm one of the Phelps disasters. He'll talk, Michael. Think of what a damn good story it'll make. I'll never work again."

Spraggue rested his hand on her shoulder. She shuddered at the touch.

"Please," she said. "Just a chance. I'll do whatever you say. You can stay with me every minute. Lock me in a closet except for rehearsals—"

"Darien ought to know."

"Even if I'm not the joker?" She licked her dry lips, swallowed audibly. "Of course, if you believe my grandfather's ghost is

102

causing all the commotion, enraged by my presence in his theater, then firing me would stop the whole mess."

"Do you have a phone?"

"Down the hall."

The phone call took only two minutes. Georgina looked up as he entered the room again.

"I'll wait outside while you get dressed and pack a bag," he said. "You're staying with my aunt until I find out whether you're lying."

"You didn't call Darien," she said incredulously. "You didn't call him and you didn't call the police."

"No."

She stood on tiptoes and lightly kissed his chin. He felt as if he'd been licked by a wag-tailed puppy.

"Pack a bag," he said sternly. "I'll put you in a taxi."

"But you won't tell. . . ."

"Not yet, Georgie. Not yet."

Chapter Seventeen

Spraggue walked the mile and a half back to the theater. Breathe in for four counts, hold for eight, breathe out for eight. Two blocks of that and his head felt clear again.

Georgina: guilty or innocent? Guilty: hell of a motive; concealment of her background; secrecy about the decapitated doll. No. That wouldn't play. If Georgina had planned the doll bit, she'd have shouted her injury from the rooftops . . . unless she was subtler than he thought. Innocent: he wanted her to be.

If someone else—X, the joker—had broken into Georgie's place, he'd be a fool not to use the material it offered. So the joker could have planned on making Georgie a scapegoat, knowing her background from the silent witness of her room. Even the poster was there, a standout: Samuel Borgmann Phelps presents *Macbeth.*

Georgina *could* have planted the doll herself. Maybe there had been no doll, just a story to match Deirdre's. But then, couldn't that be said of all the other pranks? Was anyone in the clear?

The trick that had brought him in: Frank Hodges's Bloody Mary banquet, for instance. Frank could have had a secret penchant for drinking blood. Or he could have tipped back his regular vodka-and-tomato-juice and put on a performance for Darien. Had to remember he was dealing with actors. Why would Frank fake it? To get out of the show. Why? To be able to harass the cast more freely. Obstacle: Frank was safely in New York. Or was he? Spraggue had dialed a New York number, heard a voice on the phone, no more. Frank's motive? A blank; none known.

What about the other jokes? The tricks seemed to group themselves effortlessly. The decapitated dolls, the sculpted, bloody head of Gregory Hudson, the blood bath. None of the victims injured in any way. Victim and perpetrator could be one and the same in every case. The bucket of blood, hung up for Emma. Delayed action, so the redheaded seductress could have set it herself, stepped deftly aside at the last moment, screamed effectively. The trip wire. Again, set up beforehand. For Caroline—or Emma. By Caroline or Emma. Neither could be eliminated.

Eddie's case—slightly different. Eddie had made actual contact with the joker. Ruled him out, right? Wrong. The entire episode could be fabrication. What evidence did Eddie have to back up his claims? The writing on the walls, the wrecked apartment created by Eddie himself? The balancing act on the chair, the rope burns—would the joker go so far as to inflict wounds on himself? *If* he were crazy enough, or committed enough. Spragque saw no reason to doubt either possibility.

That left the actors who had not been annoyed by X—yet: John Langford and Gustave Grayling. If the tricks were being performed in the same order as Dracula's attacks on his victims, wouldn't that tend to cast suspicion on the leading man? Spragque smiled as he recalled the great actor's "psychological" insights. Either the man was an idiot. . . .

No. Not stupid. A fine actor, and that took intelligence—an instinctive, narrow brilliance, an imitative gift. Spragque had known extraordinary actors who were hardly safe outside the theater, but he would never have called them stupid.

An illusionist; that's who he was up against, a master of disguise and misdirection. Both he and Eddie had actually seen the joker, the mysterious X. What could either say about him?

Eye color. . . . Why hadn't he concentrated on that with the joker only twenty feet away? Eye color, height, weight: those were the things the police wanted to know first in any description, the immutables. How immutable in an actor?

Then there were the nonactors: Darien and Dennis Boland, the Spider. And Karen. Spragque quickened his step.

He overtook the Boylston Street pedestrians, the brightly dressed summer tourists and the harried lunch-break shoppers. Envied the hand-holding couples at the sidewalk cafés. Passed the Copley Square fountain, the library, the Prudential Center. Rounded the corner at Mass Ave, pressed on. No time for lunch. No time for—

He heard running steps behind him, turned, and almost collided with Eddie Lafferty.

"Geez, you walk fast!" The company's madman was breathing hard. Beads of perspiration dotted his forehead, dripped onto his round, hornrimmed glasses. "Darien was looking for you right before break."

"Sounds ominous." Spraggue started walking again, slower. Eddie matched his stride.

"I was hoping to find you, too." Lafferty hesitated. "I wanted to thank you for what you did at my apartment."

"You already did."

"And . . . um . . . I had no idea Arthur hired you to find the joker."

"Eddie." Spraggue stopped and faced Lafferty, trying to pin down the elusive blue eyes. "How did you see that trip wire? You never wear your glasses in the theater."

"Um . . . no, I don't. It's . . . uh . . . a character thing. I see Renfield as sort of an unfocused being, so I—"

"You saw that trip wire from at least ten feet away."

"The light bounced right off it! Really. It was just one of those freak things."

"You didn't know it was there?"

"Of course not. If I'd set it, why would I spoil it by warning Caroline? That's what I wanted to talk to you—shit."

"What's wrong?"

"Watch out. Here she comes."

Spraggue spun around. Caroline Ambrose half-ran behind him on spindly high heels, fast closing the gap.

"Stick around," Spraggue whispered to Eddie, pleading. The young actor grinned, blue eyes wide and slightly vacant.

"Darling!" Caroline caught at Spraggue's arm. "I'm breathless from pursuing you."

Spraggue further shortened his step, but said nothing.

"And Eddie," the star prattled on. "Did I thank you for saving my life, darling?" She wove an arm through Eddie's, caught up Spraggue with the other, skillfully arranging a threesome. Spraggue had to admire her technique: herself in the middle, a man on each arm, she prepared to approach the theater.

Eddie mumbled vaguely. Caroline took it for consent. "I'm glad. It's a wonder I remember my own name sometimes! Of course, on stage it's different. I never forget a line, never forget a cue." Caroline giggled, flashed perfect teeth. "But I shouldn't interrupt you two, I know." She smiled up at Eddie. "I'll bet you're helping Michael solve the company mystery!"

Neither man spoke. She giggled again.

"No need for alarm. I'm very discreet. I did tell you, Michael, about my dressing room? Turned topsy-turvy with all my powder upset on the floor. Very expensive powder. I have it made up specially; my skin is so sensitive. Just the sort of thing a spiteful, jealous—"

"You think the joker's a woman?"

Caroline was elated by Eddie's response. It followed her script exactly. She smiled vivaciously, first at Eddie, then at Spraggue, posing for some imaginary photographer.

"Well, I'm sure I don't know," Caroline said gravely.

They turned the corner at Huntington Avenue. She peered ahead anxiously. Spraggue and Lafferty exchanged glances. They understood the plot. The three of them were to arrive, supposedly back from a delightful lunch, laughing and bright, right under John Langford's nose. If Emma were present, so much the better. Caroline must have been lurking in a shop, waiting for a likely male to pass by. She'd gotten two—a bonus.

She chattered on as Spraggue held the door. Eddie ushered her into the theater. She kept a tight grip on his arm.

"These fake torches always make me think I've just walked into a scene from *Macbeth*," Eddie said dreamily.

Spraggue watched him curiously.

"Don't say that," Caroline said sharply. "Bad luck. Never mention the Scottish play inside a theater!"

"You believe in that?" Spraggue asked innocently.

"I was brought up in theaters. I never whistle in my dressing room, either. Silly, isn't it?"

Their entrance went unnoticed, much to Caroline's chagrin. John and Emma had not returned, ergo Caroline was not prepared to let the men go. She clung with stubborn persistence.

"I have hot water in my dressing room," she cooed. "Coffee and tea. And I hate to be alone. I'd feel so much *safer*."

She'd feel safe enough as soon as Langford returned and got an eyeful of Miss Popularity. She simpered at Eddie, who'd stepped ahead into the dressing room.

"Turn on the light, darling. To the right. And watch out for Wolf. He's sleeping. I left him in my little basket—"

"Don't come in!" Eddie's voice was choked, a barely controlled whisper.

Spraggue turned Caroline around by the shoulders, held her. "Take her into my dressing room, Eddie. Stay there."

"It's the dog." Eddie made a retching noise and ran down the hall. Blessedly, Caroline followed.

The brown-and-white terrier that had caused such a fuss at rehearsal was laid out on the dressing table in front of Caroline's gilt-edged mirror. His still body was horribly elongated. A pool of blood surrounded him, dyeing the white orchids carefully arranged on his breast. His throat was slit from side to side, almost severing his head from his body.

Spraggue slammed the door as he left. He passed Eddie in the hallway, horribly sick on the gray stone floor. He averted his head, the bile rising in his throat, and hurried out into the sunlight.

The phone booth was empty. He dialed his aunt's number, surprised at the steadiness of his fingers. Pierce answered promptly.

"Mrs. Hillman's residence."

"Is she back from lunch yet?" Spraggue asked quickly.

"No. May I take a message?"

"Georgina, the girl I told you about, is she there?"

"No."

Damn. Spraggue held up his left hand, stared at his watch. She should have arrived.

"Pierce, this is important. When Georgina gets there, question her. Make her write out a timetable, everything she did since she left me."

"Is there any trouble?"

"Never mind. Just make a note of the number of the cab she arrives in. Okay?"

"Certainly."

"Write this down. I put her in a Yellow Cab at twelve forty-five. Number 5503. If she arrives in any other cab, try to get ahold of Yellow 5503. Find out where he dropped her, if he waited, anything."

"I will. And a Lieutenant Hurley has been trying to get in touch with you."

"Thanks, Pierce. I'll phone him."

"Would you like Mrs. Hillman to return your call?"

"No. Just tell her I'll see her tonight."

Tonight. The pre-opening gala! Spraggue closed his eyes.

"Good-bye, then."

"Thanks, Pierce."

The butler hung up. Spraggue stood with the receiver in his hand for some time, thinking. Someone tapped on the booth, hoping to use the phone. Spraggue shook his head and the man stumped angrily away.

Chapter Eighteen

Spraggue hesitated, fingered the dial. 911: Police Emergency. The impulse to call, to ignore Darien's injunction, was strong. To report what? A mutt's murder? Warnings couched in blank verse? And when the police questioned him about suspects . . . was he ready to sic them on Georgina? Not yet.

He called Hurley instead. The phone rang ten times and Spraggue was about to hang up when someone lifted the receiver.

"Hurley," snapped an angry voice, muffled by a hurried swallow.

"Lunchtime, huh?"

"Spraggue? Damn right. I get fifteen minutes to stuff a sandwich down my gut and—"

"Have you got something for me?"

"Uh huh."

Spraggue had a quick mental image of the policeman, shoulder hunched against the phone, sandwich squashed in his left hand, his right hand moving unerringly for the spot on an overcrowded desk where Spraggue's information resided.

"You're working with a bunch of honeys, you know." Hurley gave a snort of laughter. "Dennis Boland's got a rap sheet as long as my arm—petty stuff, bad checks. Gregory Hudson: fag bust in New York—"

"Did you get the stuff on Darien's auto smash?"

"Yeah, sure. That and the Ambrose dame's first hubby's death certificate. The Darien stuff was tough to find, you know. No charges filed. I had to convince some young ass in New York to ferret through the beef sheets. Must have been a mess—that many years ago."

"So I owe you, Fred."

"Yeah, that's what I figure. How about paying off with some tickets to your show? I mentioned it to my wife; she's crazy about that Langford guy—"

Spraggue thought a moment, said, "How'd you like to come to a special preview tomorrow night?"

"Tomorrow night? We'd have to get a sitter."

"Get one, Fred," Spraggue said earnestly. "How's this? I'll send over a dozen passes. Hand 'em out to off-duty cops. A goodwill gesture."

"Sure it is, Spraggue. Why don't you hire a private security force?"

"Look, nothing's going to happen, Hurley."

"But if it does—"

"Having you there will give me a warm, secure feeling."

"Great," Hurley said.

"Think it over. You working tonight?"

"Yeah."

"Can you hang onto those reports until a little before eight o'clock? Then put them in a cab and send them over to my place on Fayerweather Street. Okay?"

"Will do."

"See you tomorrow," Spraggue said. He hung up, left the booth, and entered the theater by the employees' entrance on Huntington Avenue, just ten feet down from the huge main doors, but practically hidden by an overhanging alcove and Greek columns. He took the steps to Darien's office two at a time, entered without knocking.

"Where've you been?" Darien began angrily.

"Even snoops get a lunch break."

"Have you made any progress? Are you getting any closer? That business with Caroline, if it should leak to the press—"

"That's the least of our problems," Spraggue said. He skipped over his meeting with Georgina, outlined the death of the dog. "I think it's time to call in the police."

"No. Absolutely not. Tonight's the gala. Tomorrow, dress and preview. Tuesday, the official opening. We have to make it until then!"

"Cancel the damn party, Darien. It's too dangerous."

"No. I've got people in from New York, backers, press—"

"Then we'll have to make some special arrangements."

"What do you mean? What kind of arrangements? Everything's taken care of."

"What caterers are you using?" Spraggue asked. "Rachel's?"

"They were recommended," Darien replied, bewildered.

"Good. I'll call her and set things up. One of the waiters will be my man. If he's here, and my aunt, and Karen Snow—"

"The crew's got work to do tonight, Spraggue."

"The assistant stage manager will have to handle it or there'll be no damn gala. I'll need at least three observers other than myself—"

"I'll help out."

"No offense, Arthur. I need people I *know* have nothing to do with the joker, *know* on the evidence of my own eyes."

"Have it your way, Spraggue." Darien's eyes were ice.

"Cops would be better."

"No. What do you suggest I do now?"

"Cancel rehearsal and get Caroline out of this mess."

Darien smacked his forehead. "God! Caroline! Someone'll have to make a fuss over her or she'll walk out!"

"I doubt John Langford is up for it. It's your role," said Spraggue.

"Did you leave her downstairs?" The little man practically flew toward the door. "She's probably thrown a fit!"

Spraggue followed him down the first flight of stairs, veered off at the double doors to the stage. He pulled open the right-hand door just as Karen Snow shoved it from within.

"Thanks." She had a grim look in her eyes, a bucket in her hand.

"I have to talk to you."

"Well, you'll have to follow me then. Goddamned mess! Have you seen Caroline's dressing room? She won't go in there. Says I've got to find her another room! And Eddie, the poor baby!"

Spraggue put a hand on Karen's shoulder, turned her gently around. "Just give me a minute."

"I haven't got one, Spraggue!" She shook off his hand.

"You're coming to Darien's gala tonight."

"You're kidding," she said sharply. "I've got a hundred things to do tonight. One of the fog machines is jammed—"

"The ASM's going to have to take care of it. Darien's orders. I need someone to help me keep an eye on suspects."

"Can't you get Darien to cancel the damn thing?"

"I tried."

"Of all the stupid moves! When I first laid eyes on the schedule, I called him on it. Who throws a party at a time like this? *Tonight* should be dress rehearsal, tomorrow preview! What kind of maniac wants the press at a dress rehearsal? But that's the way old Phelps used to do it, and that's the way Darien's going to do it!"

"Will you come? I'll bring you flowers and pick you up at eight-thirty."

She stiffened just the way she had when he'd suggested an after-rehearsal ice-cream cone. "I'm allergic to flowers," she said, "I've got nothing to wear, and I'll walk."

"Sorry. I always seem to say the wrong thing to you."

She stared down at the floor, shook her head. "No. I'm sorry. This isn't a very good time for me."

"But I did say the wrong thing."

She smiled briefly. "At least you haven't asked me why I decided to become a stage manager. Most guys try that one within the first ten seconds."

"Why did you—"

"Spraggue!"

He smoothed back a wayward strand of her dark hair. "Find me a box and I'll take care of the dog."

"Would you? I'm worried about Eddie. I think he should go home."

Damn. Still Eddie. Always Eddie.

"Darien's canceling the afternoon rehearsal. Send the kid on his way," Spraggue said.

"Thank God." The stage manager breathed a sigh of relief. "With everybody out of here, we'll have a chance to get ready for tonight!"

They walked slowly down the corridor toward a storage room. Karen found a large flat box, heavy cardboard. "Do you want gloves?" she asked hesitantly, a shudder showing her distaste for his task.

"My hands wash easier," Spraggue said.

Caroline's dressing room was as he'd left it, light off and door closed. He lifted the dog's carcass carefully into the box. The orchids stayed in position, stuck in the partially congealed blood. He closed the cover. It reminded him of the bat, the beheaded bat in the birthday-wrapped box. But on a much larger scale.

He thought of Georgina as he washed his hands in Caroline's sink. Where had she been? If she'd gone straight to Mary's, he'd have an alibi for one more.

Caroline's delicately scented soap was having no effect on his stained hands. He sprinkled on harsh scouring powder and scrubbed. "'What, will these hands ne'er be clean?'" he murmured absently.

Macbeth. He jerked his dripping hands from the sink. "Who would have thought a dog had so much blood in him?" To paraphrase. He hunted around the room, even searching the dog's now cold and repugnant corpse. No note. No message. What in hell was the joker trying to say?

And to whom?

Chapter Nineteen

Late. Dammit, he was late. After eight o'clock and Darien's bash scheduled to begin at nine. Spraggue knotted his tie and checked his reflection in the mirror. Not that any of Darien's carefully chosen society guests would deign to arrive on time. Where in hell was that cab?

He dialed Hurley's phone number, slammed the receiver down after ten rings. He stood immobile, hand on the phone, his shirt a glistening white contrast to his elegant black trousers.

He ran swiftly through a mental checklist. The caterers: that was taken care of. Rachel had been near hysterics at the thought of Pierce decked out in her waiter's livery. But Pierce had been amenable. He'd be a credit to Rachel's steadily growing reputation for great pastry and prompt service. Aunt Mary had been bubbly, eager to get off the phone and dress for the party, but worried about Georgina's reluctance to attend. Mary, at least, would keep her head and follow instructions. Or exceed them.

Karen. She'd sounded odd on the phone, rebellious and remote. Had she been waiting for a call from someone else? Would she arrive at the party escorted by Eddie? Hell, she'd do her job. She might not be romantically inclined in his direction, but she was reliable.

A raucous horn shattered the peace on the street below. Spraggue shrugged into his dinner jacket, straightened an unruly lock of dark hair. He'd do. No John Langford, of course. He smiled as he raced down the stairs. A plum-colored jacket with a spangled cummerbund, that's what Langford would probably turn up in.

The cabbie was in the vestibule, searching for the right doorbell. He wore a doeskin cap pushed down over deep-set eyes and carried a thick Manila envelope under his arm. Spraggue grabbed him by the elbow and propelled him out the door, relieving him of the envelope and outlining the next step of the journey as the cab got underway.

The driver understood the word hurry. Spraggue averted his eyes as they shot through Harvard Square. He fumbled in his pocket and withdrew the tiny flashlight he kept on his keyring with the picklocks. The Manila envelope was carefully sealed. He broke the wax.

Twenty pages of thin onionskin paper, typed, single-spaced; Hurley had done a thorough check. Spraggue skimmed through the pages as the cab sped down Mass Ave, over the Harvard Bridge into Boston. Slipped in with the loose pages, he found two long mailing envelopes, labeled: AMBROSE DECEASE, 1968, and DARIEN ACCIDENT, 1974. He opened the first, spread the folded pages out on his lap, scanned them with the flashlight.

The Ambrose envelope contained only two sheets of paper, clipped together and folded. The top sheet was a photostat copy: *State of Illinois Medical Examiner's Certificate of Death.* *Registration District Number* and *State File Number* followed. An unevenly spaced, labeled grid informed that Ambrose, Geoffrey C., had been a white American of sixty-seven years when he'd died in the county of Cook, city of Chicago, on December 4, 1968. Married. *Name of Surviving Spouse (maiden name if wife):* Caroline Comeau. Was it maiden name? Or stage name? He skipped over *Address, Social Security Number, U.S. War Veteran (Yes, No),* down to the middle of the page. Number 18: *Death Was Caused By:* followed by the admonition to enter only one cause per line for (A), (B), and (C). (A) was labeled *Immediate Cause.* In a half-legible scrawl it said: "Arteriosclerotic Cardiovascular Disease." The next column, labeled *Approximate Interval Between Onset and Death,* was blank. So was item 18B: *Due To Or As a Consequence Of.* So was 18C: *Other Significant Conditions.* At least there was no doubt about item 19A. *Autopsy (Yes, No)* had a large clear "No" printed under it. Item 20A was also adamant: *Accident, Suicide, Homicide, or Undetermined (Specify)* had been answered with the one word, "Natural."

Spraggue stared at the piece of paper. Three sections. The first section, personal information, was completely filled out. The third, burial information, likewise. The second part, the part dealing with cause of death, was far less crowded. Out of nineteen possible bits of information, only three were listed.

118

He sighed. How many deaths had there been in Cook County on December 4, 1968? A sixty-seven-year-old man dies of a heart attack. Fill out the forms and bury the remains. So what?

What had there been to gossip about? Caroline, forty years younger than poor deceased hubby, probably hadn't mourned sufficiently. Spraggue read the burial information. Item 24A *Burial, Cremation, Removal (Specify)*. The single word "cremation" underneath. That put an effective end to speculation. Once the corpse was reduced to ash. . . .

Spraggue flipped the page. The second sheet was filled with Hurley's hastily scrawled commentary.

Mike,

Illuminating, huh? Once I got the sheet, I called the M.E. Naturally the guy who filled out this one in '68 is dead. But the guy I got was the old guy's assistant, and he remembered the doc telling him the story. You'll see why. It seems they found the old boy naked in his bed, after one of his kids had called the police. The kid had tried calling Daddy like she did every night at ten o'clock. This time, no answer.

Ambrose was D.O.A., had a history of heart trouble. No problems; they fill out the sheet. No problems, that is, until the kid and the widow get together. Big scene right at the M.E.'s office. Kid says: Where were you? Widow says: I went to the movies after tucking in hubby at eight-thirty. Kid says (and this is exactly what he told me): So how come there's semen on the sheets? You know Daddy wasn't supposed to— Ruckus ensues with daughter yelling that Caroline fucked her father to death. The new M.E. says that that's the way he wants to go! Me, too.

-H.

Underneath Hurley listed the name of the M.E. he'd spoken to, the name and address of Geoffrey Ambrose's daughter, and a column of long-distance phone charges. Spraggue stuffed the material back in its envelope.

The cab was stuck in traffic near Boylston Street. Get out and walk or take the extra time to check the second envelope? The guests would be late, Spraggue told himself. No one would show until nine-thirty at the earliest.

He slit the envelope marked DARIEN ACCIDENT, 1974, and emptied the contents on his lap. Several photostats and a page of Hurley's scrawl.

The scrawl was clipped on top: "Mike, I'll let you sort this mess out yourself! —H." That was all.

The copies were bad, lined, light in places, dark in others, as if the originals had been folded, crumpled, and desultorily smoothed before entry into the machine. Four pages in all: an accident report, a charge sheet, a death certificate, and a statement retracting charges. Spraggue's eyes followed the erratic pinpoint of his flashlight as the cab alternately raced and jerked to sudden halts. Nothing new, nothing new . . . except names. A cast of characters.

The name "Dennis" leaped out of the circle of light. Spraggue stopped reading, went back. Dennis Boland listed as a witness to the accident. Spraggue checked the time and place of the accident: early morning, 3 A.M.; a heavily trafficked intersection. With fat Spider conveniently lurking on the corner? He turned the page.

Another death certificate, from the State of New York this time, but remarkably similar. Alison Arnold, female, 22, resident of the City of New York. Died of massive injuries caused by automobile accident.

Massive injuries. And what were those? Code words to spare sensitive eyes? No punctured lungs, no twisted limbs and bloody flesh. Just "massive injuries," the end.

So much for Alison Arnold. Spraggue shoved the page aside angrily. Why not an unusual last name, a small-town birthplace? Ambrose's daughter would be easy to check on, name and address thoughtfully included in Hurley's report. But where would he find the relatives of Alison Arnold, seven years dead?

Why try to find those people at all? Why raise up those buried ghosts? If the joker's motive were revenge. . . . But if revenge, why the messages from *Macbeth*? *Hamlet* was the revenge play. Or *The Spanish Tragedy*. Why *Macbeth*?

Spraggue's finger stabbed at the next page, a complaint against Arthur L. Darien: drunken driving. And the charge: vehicular homicide, not the more common manslaughter. Someone had been out for Darien's blood. The signature on the complaint form was cramped, but the name was neatly typed beneath: Albert W. Arnold—and an address! The Arnolds wouldn't be so hard to locate, after all.

Spraggue thumbed the pages. There was no investigative report. None—just a single, signed document in which Albert Arnold agreed to dismiss all charges against Arthur Darien.

"Okay if I drop you here?" The cabbie's voice broke into his

120

reverie. "I could turn down Huntington, but if you're in a hurry—"

Quarter to nine. Spraggue slid all the papers back into the envelope, paid up, and hurried across the street.

Chapter Twenty

The theater, Spraggue thought, was decked out like a high school gym before a prom. Darien had loosed florists in the double-tiered lobby. A late-summer riot of blooms brightened the somber foyer. Red-coated waiters scurried silently, clutching heavy silver trays. Chandeliers gleamed off crystal stemware. Spraggue straightened his tie.

Only a few of the unfashionably early were present, along with Spraggue's lieutenants. Aunt Mary carried a purse big enough to house Hurley's collected notes. A photographer fussed with his equipment. From the lower lobby came the hum of tuning instruments.

Gradually, the actors made their entrances, selected their vantage points.

Caroline Ambrose, in shimmering aqua, seemingly recovered from the adventures of the afternoon, held court on the curved staircase leading up to the first balcony. There, she draped herself advantageously against a carved pillar, a rococo gilded cherub ogling her low-cut bodice, a spray of orchids in her hair. A procession of dinner-jacketed, gray-templed men, all clearly labeled FINANCIAL BACKER, attended her.

Langford had bowed to Spraggue as he entered, flashing that dazzling smile. Plum-colored velvet, all right, but no cummerbund; a waistcoat, embroidered in blues, purples, and magenta, with just a touch of gold thread. "Getting closer to our ghost, I hope," Langford had muttered. In response to Spraggue's nod, he'd beamed. "Good. I was afraid you might be too late." Then, without breaking stride, he'd continued over to the far smoking lounge where he now posed between the fireplace and the lily pool. He entertained the backers' wives, smiling brilliantly at the elderly females, raising a relieved eyebrow when Emma, in incredibly tight strapless red, offered to refresh his champagne glass. Among Langford's coterie, Spragque picked out the variegated hair of his aunt. She'd insisted that Langford be one of "her" charges.

Now she turned, caught his eye, and started through the crowd. They met under the central chandelier.

"Lovely party!" she said loudly, then under her breath, "Stand close. I have to whisper! Smile!"

"Is that so," said Spragque in a teasing voice, moving nearer and grinning for the benefit of the other guests.

"First," his aunt said, "Georgina. She arrived in a different cab than the one you sent her off in. Pierce spoke to both drivers. Details in here." She pressed a small envelope into his hand. "Briefly, she seems to have wandered around the Prudential Center for half an hour."

Half an hour. Ten minutes' walk to the theater, ten minutes back. She could have done it, but just barely.

"The cabbie who picked her up at the Pru," Spragque said, "did he say anything about her?"

"Like?"

"Like she seemed upset or—"

"Nothing." Aunt Mary shook her head vigorously.

"Did she have any blood on her clothes when she got to you?"

"Certainly not! Michael, she's a lovely child. I'm sure she had nothing to do with—"

"Just keep an eye on her, Aunt Mary."

"I will," Aunt Mary said firmly. She twined her arm through his and they walked slowly toward the foyer, keeping careful smiles on their lips, nodding to passersby. "Now pay attention, Michael," she said when everyone was out of earshot. "This part is intriguing. I had lunch with Jamie Blakeley."

Spragque's eyes glittered. "That was intriguing?"

"Not in itself. But he did give me the names of his fellow backers. I've been chatting around all day and I collared the holdouts this evening. And it just doesn't add up."

"What doesn't?"

"The money, Michael! All the folks I've spoken to are only token investors, a few thousand here and there. The totals don't add up to half enough to mount this kind of a show. If what you've told me is true—scenery from New York, designer costumes, salaries—well, my dear, all I can say is there must be another angel determined to stay in the dark. None of the backers know who he is."

"That is intriguing," Spraggue murmured.

"Thought you might find it so. Back to my post now, dear. It really *is* a lovely party."

"Have you tried the *Macbeth* bit with Langford?"

"Haven't had a chance to get a word in edgewise, Michael. Those women are so bold!"

"Keep trying."

"I shall."

Spraggue watched as she wound her way back through the crowd. A hidden backer. . . . He scanned the room.

Greg Hudson seemed to have brought along a boyfriend, a dark, bearded fellow Spraggue had never seen before. The man shifted uncomfortably in his dinner jacket. Had he been picked up for the occasion and hurriedly stuffed into rented clothes? To annoy Emma? To make her feel sorry for Greg? Hudson was drinking too much. Waiters, trays heavily laden with champagne glasses, rarely got by him untouched.

Gus Grayling was resplendent, brushed and polished to a burnished shine, exuding a faint air of stage nobility. He flirted with the older women, but kept an arm possessively around Georgina's waist. Spraggue raised an eyebrow. Langford's plan seemed to have worked. At intervals, Grayling checked the crowd around the leading man and smiled whenever it thinned out. Once he waved over at Langford, taking great care that John should see Georgina.

The tiny blonde looked frozen, brittle. Her worried eyes never relaxed. She knew about Caroline's dog; she'd denied the deed emphatically, offered to take a polygraph test. Spraggue wondered how a lie detector would handle actors. Surely those who lied as a profession could effectively fool a machine.

Laughter and music bubbled up from the downstairs lounge. The largest of the front-of-house areas, it was a natural ballroom. The dais, where refreshments were sold during intermission, was now a miniature stage for a tightly packed combo.

Spraggue fastened a polite smile on his face and escaped from Mrs. Perlmutter, patroness of the arts. He wished the damned shindig would end. Too many people. Too many he knew, too many who knew him. His smile felt stretched to the breaking point.

Moving through the crowd in the downstairs lounge, he barely nodded to an observant, red-coated Pierce on the landing.

The crush was greater here, the mist of cigar and cigarette smoke more foully potent.

Deirdre Marten stood alone in a corner, tapping her foot to the rhythm. Spraggue doubted she'd dance much. In stark black, she looked too pure, too untouchable. No matter how attracted by her beauty, a man would hesitate to approach the ice princess. Was she still waiting for her chance to take over Emma's role? Did she still believe another "incident" would happen?

Who would Deirdre play in *Macbeth*? One of the witches, if the director saw the trio as deadly and cold. Or a young Lady Macbeth in that stiff black gown. But none of the companies Deirdre Marten or Dinah Martowski worked with had done *Macbeth*. She was one of the few Aunt Mary had been able to check on thoroughly. No unexplained gaps in her acting career.

Aunt Mary. . . . She kept careful watch upstairs. Pierce lurked on the steps. And Karen— Spraggue saw her even as he had the thought. She was dancing with Eddie Lafferty.

Her deep blue dress suited her. Spraggue found its voluminous folds more intriguing than Emma's half-bared bosom.

Karen and Eddie danced well, but there was distance between them. Eddie, Spraggue decided, held back. Fear of older women? Natural reserve? Spraggue waited until the tune was finished, tapped Karen lightly on the shoulder, and led her back out to the floor. If he said nothing, she couldn't refuse.

"Look like you're having a good time," he whispered.

"Why?" Rebellion flared in her eyes.

"Did you talk to Eddie about *Macbeth*?"

"I've got work to do, Spraggue!"

"Michael. Did you ask him?"

"Yes," she whispered furiously. "He *loves* the play, but he's *never* been in it. And he didn't curl up and act sinister when I mentioned it!"

"Relax," Spraggue said gently. "Smile."

"I'm uncomfortable. They all know I shouldn't be here!"

"You look like you wear long gowns and go dancing every night of the week. The cast will just assume that Eddie brought you."

"He didn't."

Spraggue tightened his arm around her. "Good."

"I'm serious. I'm the only techie here."

"Dennis Boland's coming down the stairs."

"Him! He's Darien's shadow."

"Odd sort of shadow," Spraggue answered speculatively.

"He is odd." Karen looked up at Spraggue quizzically. "He's a good house manager, efficient as hell. But can you picture him as Darien's best friend? Darien's such a snob, really. Look at him, beaming at all the Beacon Hill people, fawning on the press. He could be upstairs now, sharing center stage with John Langford, and instead he's down here with fat little Dennis. Lunches with fat little Dennis. Dines with fat little Dennis. I can't see my Arthur Darien being *kind*. Don't you wonder what keeps them together?"

"Very much. Darien seems in a good mood tonight." He whispered so that she'd have to draw even closer. Her dark, sleek hair came up just past his chin. It smelled like lilies-of-the-valley.

"Why not? Some of the reviewers here tonight are the same ones who drove him out of the business five years ago."

"They could still pan us tomorrow."

She smiled, shook her head. "This play has an aura of success about it." Her smile faded nervously. "If nothing else happens."

The music stopped. They applauded and stood off to one side, watching Arthur Darien.

"He hasn't had a drink all evening," Karen said suddenly. "I've been watching him."

"Did you expect him to get roaring drunk?"

"It was just something someone said."

"Eddie?"

"Maybe."

Spraggue changed the subject. "Darien's done *Macbeth*, hasn't he?"

Karen took a step away. "I don't know. . . . Why don't you ask him?" Her dark eyes were very far away.

"I think I will."

But he didn't get the chance. He felt a hand on his shoulder, light but firm. "Dance with me," said Emma Healey. Her smile was taut. Annoyed that he hadn't asked her? Irritated that he hadn't taken notice of her slinking staircase descent?

The music started. Emma pressed her body tightly against Spraggue's and swayed. She didn't lead; she didn't follow. She molded herself to him, danced as if they were one.

She looked up. "I hardly know you," she said. "That's too bad. I try very hard to get acquainted with all my leading men—"

"You seem to know John Langford pretty well," said Spraggue.

It wasn't the response she wanted. "Oh, John." She waved him away. "John is upstairs playing matinee idol. It bores me. And John's not my only leading man in this show. You and I have love scenes. I like to know a lot about a man before I romance him onstage."

"Such as?"

"Whether he's a good dancer," she said after a pause. "You are."

"Is that important?"

"It can be."

"There's not much more to know about me."

"Michael." She lowered her eyes. She made his name sound like an endearment she had invented just for him. "I've heard a lot about you."

"What you hear may be exaggerated."

"I'd like to find out," she said playfully.

Would you now, thought Spraggue. Or would you rather find out what I know about the joker?

"You joined us so late," she went on, her lips a half-pout. "You and I have never had a chance . . . to talk." Another couple brushed by them. Emma pressed closer. "I hate crowds," she said with a sigh. "And parties like this give me a pain. Just sucking up to the press. And the backers are mostly dirty old men. Why don't we leave, you and me?"

"And go where?"

"Wherever you want. Your place. Mine."

Spraggue shook his head regretfully, ran his hand down her spine. The red dress had no zipper. How did she get into it? Or, better yet, out of it? "Sorry. I can't leave."

"Can't?" Her eyebrows arched.

"I'm on duty, Emma. Keeping watch for the joker."

"The party has to end."

"What about John?" Spraggue asked.

Emma laughed. "He doesn't own me. John will be going off to some other frightful event. A cocktail party at one of the backers' homes. I'd love to miss it."

The song ended. Emma pressed a scrap of paper, hastily pulled from her tiny red bag, into his hand. "Address and phone number," she said. "I'll be waiting." She walked away.

Spraggue let out his breath. The hand that had touched the red dress felt hot, burned. What was behind this sudden seduction? A ploy to make John Langford jealous? Greg? A game to further infuriate Caroline? He slipped the piece of paper into his pocket. It might turn out to be a far better evening than he'd anticipated.

By midnight the party was acclaimed a success. The music blared louder, disco added to the more staid fare. Colors melded and swirled in a champagne haze. Caroline, Langford, and Darien stood out, stars of the evening. The ensemble chattered and danced, glossy as résumé photos.

Résumé photos. If he could just—

The lights went out. The music stopped raggedly, one reluctant clarinetist continuing long past the others. A stifled curse rang out in the sudden silence. Someone giggled. A tray overturned in a clatter of broken glassware. Then a new sound began, an eerie, thin whistle of wind.

It began indistinctly, welling up from the dance floor. The musicians stared dumbly at their instruments. The speakers had a life of their own.

The voices were whispers, high, thin, menacing—a curious singsong chant.

> "*Thrice the brinded cat hath mew'd.*
> *Thrice, and once the hedge-pig whin'd.*
> *Harpier cries; ' 'Tis time, 'tis time.'*"

"God!" It was Caroline's strangled voice. "It's *Macbeth*. Not *Macbeth*!"

"What in hell is—" Darien started strong, faded off.

"It's my recording." John Langford's tones were unmistakable. "My London recording. Who could have—"

Then came a woman's voice.

"*The thane of Fife had a wife; where is she now? — What, will these hands ne'er be clean?*" The voice rose to a shriek, ended in sobbing.

Someone dropped a glass.

Spraggue saw the thin beam, felt the cold metal of the flashlight pressed against his hand. "Trace the wire," Spraggue whispered, fixing his light on Pierce's worried face. The butler nodded. They moved noiselessly up the stairs together.

Far away, the howl of a wolf joined the wind. Underneath, music grew—harsh and menacing. A new voice spoke.

"*Rats,*" the voice said. "*Rats, rats, rats! Hundreds, thousands, millions of them, and every one a life; and dogs to eat them, and cats too. All lives! all red blood, with years of life in it—*"

Spraggue and Pierce made their way through the hushed foyer, through the employees' exit and down the steps.

"At least the bastard's quoting *Dracula* now," Spraggue said. "I'd hate to think he was terrorizing the wrong cast."

"Wiring from below," Pierce murmured. "I checked the dais. Neat little holes."

"The dressing rooms," said Spraggue.

In Gus Grayling's cubicle the two men traced the voices to their source. A massive tape recorder lay hidden by a tarpaulin, camouflaged by the overflow of ivy from a large potted plant. Wires ran up and out one of the high windows; wooden shavings indicated drilled holes. But the tape recorder, the wires, were not the central focus.

Next to the equipment was a cage, a large metal prison. Beside it, another one, also empty. Stacked on every chair, piled on the floor: cages of every possible size. A sudden noise, an animallike chirrup, made Spraggue turn. Behind the door sat another cage, average size, tiny silvery bars. But this one wasn't empty.

A single rat, red eyes burning in the flashlight glare, paced frantically back and forth. On top of the cage, neatly printed in all caps, a sign read:

RATS! HUNDREDS, THOUSANDS, MILLIONS OF THEM!
GUESS WHERE THE OTHERS ARE!

Chapter Twenty-one

"All right." Scarcely an hour later, Spraggue confronted his exhausted lieutenants in the main lobby. Aunt Mary and Pierce shared a rose velvet love seat. Karen stood nearby, tracing a pattern in the rug with one sling-backed sandal. "Tell me about *Macbeth*."

In a short time the theater had lost its feverish gala glow. Age seeped through the cracks in its makeup. Flowers drooped. Cigarette butts jammed the stinking ashtrays. The remnants of one shattered crystal glass decorated the stairway.

"Michael." Darien entered the lobby through the auditorium doors. "Those rats—" Try as he might, the director couldn't quite suppress a shudder. "When do you think—"

"The exterminators are working as quickly as they can. Thank God, all the rats don't resemble that monster in the cage. They're relatively harmless white ones." Spraggue raised his voice over the sudden hum of speculation. "Arthur, that was a nice job of crowd control. When I came upstairs, I was expecting a stampede."

Darien looked grim. "Ever had a bomb threat?"

"No."

The director summoned a halfhearted grin. "Neither have I, but we all rehearsed them in the sixties. Never thought I'd have a rat threat."

"More than a threat," Spraggue said.

"Michael?" Aunt Mary spoke up. "Aren't white rats much easier to purchase? Laboratories and such?"

"Yeah. I was wondering where our friend would pick up so many wharf rats."

"Shall I start calling around? Pet shops, scientific-supply warehouses—"

"In the morning. Right now"—Spraggue paused slightly—"I want to know about *Macbeth*."

"Shall I start?"

Spraggue nodded at his aunt.

"I was assigned," she began, peering at the small circle of faces, "both John Langford and Caroline Ambrose. I tackled Langford first. As soon as I mentioned *Macbeth*, Michael, he was off. How many times he's done it, who he's played, who he's directed in it, how he'd design it—"

"Did he mention any particular production? Any hard-luck production?"

"To hear him carry on, you'd think they were all hard-luck shows. Story after story after story."

"But no strange reactions?"

Mary pursed her lips. "Just rampant ego."

"Odd."

"What, Michael?"

"Nothing. From something John said earlier, I thought he was on to the messages. Never mind. What about Caroline?"

"Well, to begin with, she only agreed to discuss the matter if I refrained from quotation and referred to *Macbeth* as the Scottish play."

Spraggue grunted. "And?"

"She's played Lady Macbeth three times. Only the ban on quotation kept her from illustrating. No allusions to any particular production. No guilty starts or jumps."

"Hudson was mine," Spraggue said. "He's choreographed the stage fights in *Macbeth* four or five times, once for a John Langford production. Did Langford happen to mention that, Aunt Mary?"

"No."

"Have to check it out. Hudson seemed quite willing to talk about *Macbeth*, but liquor may have made him more loquacious on the subject than he would have been otherwise. Karen?"

"I told you."

"Tell the others."

"I had Eddie. He's never done *Macbeth*."

"That's it?"

"That's it." The stage manager's eyes were red-rimmed and shiny, her voice throaty with a curious gulp in it.

"Okay, Karen. You know what has to be done. You and Mary

132

and Pierce make out the timetable. I want to know where everyone was at eleven-fifteen."

"Why then?" Arthur Darien said curiously.

"Forty-five minutes of blank leader on the tape, Arthur. The fireworks began just after midnight."

"I see."

"And another time check at eleven fifty-five," Spraggue continued. "Right, Karen?"

"Whoever jammed the lights must have sneaked out around then to diddle the fuse box," she answered wearily. There was something in her voice that made Spraggue turn and regard her carefully.

"But you didn't see anyone?" he asked softly.

She hesitated for only an instant. "No."

Darien interrupted. "Michael, you know I appreciate your letting me sit in on this conference. I don't want to take up time, but could you explain something? What about the other actors? You only asked about John and Caroline and—"

Spraggue motioned the director aside. "In a minute, Arthur, I'll explain the whole thing to you. If you could wait . . . ?"

"No trouble."

"Aunt Mary?" Michael gently removed her from the corner where she huddled with Pierce and Karen, and walked her slowly across the room. "I'm planning to sleep in Brookline tonight. But don't wait up for me. I'll be late."

"All right."

"When you've finished the timetable, have Pierce call a cab. And take Karen home on your way."

"Does that young woman usually tell the truth?" Mary asked.

"I think so."

"She didn't tonight. Not when she said she'd noticed nothing unusual at eleven fifty-five. Her voice was different. She lowered her eyes. Classic signs."

Spraggue sighed. "Agreed."

Aunt Mary patted him on the shoulder. "I'll try to find out what's worrying her on the way home. If I do, I'll leave you a note under the jade bowl." She smiled up at him. "I think she's a very attractive person, Michael."

Spraggue, busy with his own thoughts, looked up suddenly. "Huh? Who?"

"Karen Snow, dear," Aunt Mary whispered. "I wonder why she lied."

Spraggue returned his aunt to the huddle. Darien was still waiting, impatiently pacing the carpet in the far smoking lounge.

"What do you want to know, Arthur?" Spraggue said rapidly. He hoped the wait hadn't soured the director's mood.

"I want to know why you concentrated on asking about four of the actors. Just four."

"Okay." Spraggue sat on a chair by the fireplace, rested his hands on his knees. "Emma and Gus we've ruled out on appearance. That doesn't mean they may not *know* something, but they're out of the running for the joker. And Georgina. . . ." He hesitated briefly. "I think I can rule out Georgina."

"That's good. At least we're getting somewhere."

"Deirdre's never been involved in *Macbeth*. We know that from our research."

"And why *Macbeth?*"

Spraggue stood, stared Darien straight in the eye, and said "Arthur, *you* tell *me* about *Macbeth*."

The director looked away, then spluttered, "Loathe the play. Why you should think I'd—"

"Arthur! You recognized that voice."

"That whisper? I'd be damned good if I could recognize a voice through that kind of distortion!"

"Not the whisper at the end, Darien. Not the witches at the beginning. The middle voice. You dropped your glass when you heard it."

"I was surprised. The lights had gone out."

"The lights had *been* out. You didn't drop the glass when they failed. You waited—until you heard that woman's voice."

"Wasn't it from John Langford's *Macbeth?* The one he directed in London? I don't recall who he used for Lady Macbeth—"

"No, Arthur. The witches were from the Langford production. Then the quality of the tape changed. Scratchier. An amateur effort, I'd say. Possibly old."

"I didn't notice." Darien was starting to sweat. His hands clenched and unclenched.

"What I don't understand, Arthur," Spraggue said mildly, "is why you don't want to help me. It can't be in your best interest to make this show fail."

"In *my* interest!" Darien shook his head, stared at the ground. "I know the voice," he said bitterly.

134

"*Knew* the voice, don't you mean. It is Alison Arnold?"

"Spraggue, I had nothing to do with that woman's death. The brakes failed on my car." Darien was sweating in earnest now. "I could have been killed as easily as she. There were witnesses—"

"Dennis Boland?"

"Yes. That's how I met Dennis." The director spoke rapidly, as if his mouth were dry.

"You directed Alison Arnold in *Macbeth*?"

"The play was never presented. After her death—she was a total unknown, Spraggue. I was taking a terrific chance using her—"

"And you were drinking then."

"I was *not* drunk that night! And I've never taken a drink, that day to this—"

"Arthur." Spraggue stopped him with a glance. "Why didn't you tell me this before?"

"Tell you what? I had no idea until I heard that tape tonight. Even then, I was hoping I was wrong, mistaken. I would have said something—in private—later."

"You didn't know about the *Macbeth* messages?" Spraggue's tone was frankly skeptical.

"I didn't know the messages were from *Macbeth*. I hate the play! I've forgotten the play! I don't think about *Macbeth*!"

"You're going to have to," Spraggue said coldly. "First, Arthur, I think you should have protection. More protection than I can offer you. If you won't go to the police, hire a private bodyguard."

Darien didn't speak. He just shook his head.

"You're in danger, Arthur."

"If *I'm* in danger, *I'll* take care of it, Spraggue."

"Okay. I'll need a list of everyone involved in that production of *Macbeth*. Get it to Pierce before you leave the theater." Spraggue checked his watch. No way he could start investigating until tomorrow morning. He felt in his pocket. The slip of paper Emma Healey had given him was still warm to the touch.

Darien was talking. "But I can't remember back that far. It was years ago."

"Try," Spraggue said firmly. "Does anyone in the cast seem at all familiar to you? You know, you can't quite remember where you've seen that face before?"

"No." The director shook his head. "Why?"

Spraggue raised one eyebrow. "Because," he said, "I have a strong feeling that one of your actors is related to Alison Arnold."

Chapter Twenty-two

Emma was living on Marlborough Street, in a sublet apartment in a typical Back Bay brownstone. The door opened promptly on his first ring. She didn't ask for identification.

She had changed clothes. He would never find out how she wriggled out of that red dress. The outfit she'd put on had been designed to be gotten out of easily—loose, silky, ice-blue pajamas, tied at the waist.

The blue cooled her fiery hair. Stretched out on a shabby sofa, she looked relaxed, but one bare foot tapped a nervous rhythm. The room was lit only by candles.

"Romantic," commented Spraggue. He took off his tie, stuffed it in his jacket pocket.

"Take off your jacket, too," she said, eyes amused. "I use candlelight precisely because the place *isn't* very romantic. It's all I could find. I hate hotels."

Spraggue tossed his jacket on a chair, sat near her on the couch.

She lit a cigarette, put it out after a glance at Spraggue's face. "You don't like women who smoke?"

"I don't like *anyone* to smoke before I kiss them."

She tossed the pack of cigarettes on an end table. "And unlike my friend, Gregory, you kiss only women. . . . How nice."

"What about your friend, John?" Spraggue said.

She looked at him speculatively. "I like what you do with Seward."

"How about what I do with Spraggue?"

"I don't know. You're still a mystery. Tell me, what do you think of our last scene together?"

"Definitely your best moment," Spraggue said easily. "Vampirism becomes you."

137

"I've often thought that," she said smiling. "I love being the Woman in White. She makes the rest of Lucy—the simpy side—worth doing. For me, the climax is when I almost get you to betray Van Helsing, to join me and live forever, to let me kiss you and bite your neck." She leaned forward and ran her tongue over even, white teeth. Spragague realized how few of the buttons on her pajama top she'd bothered with. Her nipples pressed against the thin blue cloth. She moved closer.

"But I kill Lucy," he said regretfully. "A stake through her heart, through your beautiful breast."

Her smile widened. "Seward would never kill me. Van Helsing kills me. Without him, without his power over Seward, the scene would be much different."

"How different?"

She laughed delightedly. "I love to experiment."

"Was Greg Hudson one of your experiments, Emma? Do you experiment with *everyone*—or only men?"

"Does it matter?" She leaned over and started unbuttoning his shirt. "Men are much easier."

"Doesn't anyone ever refuse to play?"

"No. I enjoy that, too."

"Power, Emma. Right?"

She laughed again. "I just want to make it harder for you to drive your stake through my heart."

She untied her pajamas. They slipped off as easily as he'd thought they would.

They made love on the couch, on the floor. Emma was always inviting—receptive, passively initiating each beautifully controlled moment. Spragague felt as if he were being led through a carefully choreographed dance.

When they were through, sated, it was as if he'd never touched her.

They showered together. Emma cupped her left breast, thrust it forward to be kissed. "That's where the stake has to go," she murmured. "It will be harder to kill me now, won't it?"

"I kill the vampire. Lucy's already dead."

"But what about Emma?" she said, teasing yet serious.

"I don't understand," he said.

"You don't suspect me of being the joker now. Not after tonight."

Spragague splashed water on his face. Was this ersatz passion an exchange for excluding her from his investigation?

"I heard that tape tonight," she went on. "You can't believe that voice was mine."

"I've never heard you whisper. You're a good actress. I give you credit for that. And credit for knowing that you can't prove your innocence by screwing me."

"Couldn't I prove someone else's innocence?" she said archly.

"How?"

"If he were screwing me. . . ."

"Who?"

"John Langford. This afternoon. Here, right from rehearsal up until the party. He wouldn't have had time to set up all that stuff." She paused briefly. "How's that for an alibi?"

"Pretty good. For *both* of you."

"Of course, John *is* up to something, Michael. He won't say what, but it has nothing to do with me. I'd hate to think *I* was the cause of all this upset."

Sprague took her pointed chin in his hand. "You would *love* it, Emma. Look at all the intrigues you've already created in the cast. One of your more successful experiments."

"You find me cold?" She shrugged. "John only thinks about himself. Wouldn't it be lovely if his dismal past caught up in time to prevent him from playing the Crowning Role of His Career?"

Sprague grunted.

"You're so noncommittal, Michael."

Sprague toweled himself, started to dress. "I have to go home."

"You can sleep here."

She was incredibly beautiful, hair damp, a towel draped loosely around her. He refused; there was work to be done. But he hadn't minded being experimented on for a few hours.

He called a cab.

As he walked down the front steps ten minutes later, a small dark car pulled away suddenly.

By the time he got to his aunt's, it was five A.M. She'd left the porch light on. Sprague thanked her silently as he fumbled for his little-used key.

The handwriting on the pages, carefully folded under the jade bowl in the library, was Pierce's—the finished timetable of the suspects' evening activities. No note from Aunt Mary; she must have pried nothing out of Karen. Sprague mastered the desire to call the stage manager, but couldn't control the wish that she, not Emma, had invited him home.

Wait. There was a note in another hand, not Aunt Mary's; an unfamiliar rounded, schoolgirl scrawl. Half a torn-out note-book-page signed "Georgie."

Michael dear,
Exonerated at last! Now admit it, I couldn't have gotten all that sound stuff and bought all those rats and set the whole thing up when I was right here in your lovely house all afternoon. Your aunt, who is a darling, will alibi me.
    See how right you were to trust me? And I appreciate it, appreciate it, *appreciate it*! Believe me.

Spraggue smiled, tucked the folded sheet of paper in with Pierce's report, added them to Hurley's envelope, and headed for the kitchen. On the top shelf of the refrigerator, from a small silver tray, a frosted glass of milk and a tiny strawberry confection stared at him. Mary must have told Dora that he'd be in late.

He took the pastry and the tray, substituted a Pepsi for the soporific milk, and went up to the tower, the bedroom he'd had as a boy. He tiptoed past the south guest room. He wasn't sure where Mary had put Georgina.

In the tower, the sheets were turned down. Fresh towels and soap in the bath. Spraggue stripped off his clothes and settled into bed, stuffed two plump pillows behind his back, and turned the reading lamp on full.

Pierce's timetable was neatly margined and columned, print-ed in his tiny, precise hand. The first column, headed "Suspects," listed the cast, the director, and the house manager. The second column read: "Location at 11:15." The third: "Seen by." The fourth: "11:55." The fifth reiterated the third: "Seen by."

The "stars" of the evening had been quickly vouched for. Langford, Ambrose, Darien had ways of making their presence felt. Dennis Boland, the plump Spider, had danced attendance continuously on Darien. Emma Healey hadn't been quite so loyal to John Langford. She'd moved around a lot, but in that red dress she'd had plenty of observers. Both Mary and Pierce reported positively that she hadn't left the room.

Spraggue pulled the thin blanket up over his knees; the late summer nights were getting chilly. He stretched his arms over his head and yawned, took a long sip of his caffeine-laced drink.

The other actors, according to Pierce's table, were harder to place, less colorful. Greg Hudson, Pierce thought, had been too drunk to carry out any action needing a modicum of finesse. Deirdre, no one could place exactly. Eddie was vouched for by Karen, dancing with her. Damn . . . Gus Grayling, Mary was sure, hadn't left his clutch of admirers or released Georgina's hand for more than an instant. So much for the timetable.

The second document was in another hand, bold sweeping capitals, sprawling grandiose loops. Arthur Darien's sketchy cast list for that 1974 production of *Macbeth*. A lot of good that would do; Darien seemed to remember so little. Maybe he had blocked it out of his mind. A few of the names Sprague recognized. Darien had by no means used a cast entirely composed of unknowns. Alison Arnold had flown in exalted company. No one from Darien's *Dracula* cast had been involved in the ill-fated *Macbeth*. Sprague shrugged. He'd expected as much. A drive for revenge seven years later spoke of more than a colleague, more even than a friend. Who in the company was related to Alison Arnold?

Sprague ran the parade of suspects through his ever-sleepier mind.

Caroline. Had she a niece, a daughter named Alison? None of her husbands had been named Arnold. A niece, more likely. But she had been such a good friend of Darien's—and for so long, years before '74. *If* you believed her stories. Her tale about Darien and Spider and their shared Brooklyn boyhood, had been contradicted by Darien himself.

Langford. Was John up to something, as Emma had said? Screwing someone else in the company, determined to infuriate Caroline further? What had he meant by that remark at the party, that quick, cryptic "I was afraid you might be too late"?

Greg Hudson and Eddie Lafferty were both more likely suspects than Caroline or John. Prospective younger brothers to Alison Arnold? Had that been Greg's car out in front of Emma's apartment?

Sprague shook himself as his head fell forward. Still one more document to study: the *Dracula* script. Combination dress rehearsal–press preview tonight, and he was still unsure of several lines and cues. He'd certainly have done a great job if, despite no disturbance at the performance, the play bombed because he'd never bothered to learn his lines!

He studied until eight, then thought about breakfast. Too tired to eat. Just one phone call. Fred Hurley.

Hurley must have just gotten to his desk. Sprague could hear him slurping coffee, almost smell it over the line.

Spraggue sat up straight, tried to make his voice sound alert. "Hurley, good stuff you sent me." The detective always responded well to early-morning praise.

Hurley took time out from coffee drinking to answer, "Wait'll you get the bill!"

"Just wanted to make sure you'd received the passes."

"Yeah. Thanks. My wife's looking forward to it."

"Bring her backstage afterward."

Hurley's voice turned wary. "Sure. And I did what you said with those other passes, too. You expecting something to blow up tonight?"

"No," Spraggue said easily. "But I want to make sure."

"Okay," Hurley said gruffly. "Then I'll see you this evening. I've got work to do, you know."

"Anything on Alison Arnold's family?"

"Yeah. Telex from New York. You'll love it. Father died, mother remarried, moved out of state, name unknown."

"Great," Spraggue sighed.

"Anything else comes in, I'll call you."

"I'll be at my aunt's."

Spraggue hung up. He stretched back out on the bed. Now, if Mary could just get someone to send along those last two résumé photos. No problems with John, Caroline, Gus Grayling. They were well known; so many people could guarantee that the woman posing as Caroline Ambrose for Darien's production was the same Caroline Ambrose they'd seen on Broadway, on TV. But the others were more difficult. That man up at Theater Calgary had finally sent an old photo of Deirdre. Different hairstyle, but definitely the same person. And Emma . . . No trouble there. Everyone who'd worked with Emma Healey remembered exactly what she looked like. Spraggue indulged in some remembering, too.

The others. . . . Was Greg Hudson the real Greg Hudson? Had he done what his résumé said he'd done? Or did the résumé belong to another actor—to the *real* Gregory? And Eddie. . . . How well could he really see without his glasses? Eddie and Karen . . . Karen and Eddie. . . .

At nine o'clock, the morning of the press preview, Spraggue fell into a light, uneasy sleep.

Chapter Twenty-three

"So glad you could make it," Greg Hudson said as Spraggue sat down to apply his greasepaint. "It *is* seven o'clock; Arthur expects us in the green room at seven-fifteen, so you'd better step on it."

Spraggue ignored him, opened his makeup kit, laid out pencils and brushes in a neat row. Hudson didn't want an elaborate explanation of his sporadic rehearsal attendance any more than he wanted to know the exact number of laboratory-animal-supply houses in Boston. He just had a case of pre-performance jitters.

"Do you think my base is too pale?" Greg asked petulantly.

"Light's bad down here." Spraggue stared at Hudson critically. "Looks okay. If Darien throws up, you can change it for opening night."

"Not before some press creep writes that I look like a pasty-faced turkey."

"You don't like the critics?"

"Love 'em, love 'em all." Hudson posed in front of the mirror, adjusted his cravat, ruffled his hair. "You should have been here earlier. Fur's been flying. The great Gustave doesn't like his program credit. Wants his name up with the immortal Langford and Our Lady of the Orchids."

"Gus?" Spraggue checked his base. Good color. He hoped he'd have enough time for the spirit gum on his chin to set properly. It itched.

"I've worked with Gus before," said Hudson with a sigh. "This is general procedure. He mouses around all rehearsal, just begging you to step on him. And then when you finally *do*, he throws a tantrum. Much too late to do any good. Stalked right out of his dressing room. Called it 'a dim and nasty closet' unsuited to his position in the company."

"Where'd he go?"

"He grabbed Eddie's room. The kid was late. And when Eddie finally does walk in, he's not wearing his glasses. Method acting, you know. He sees there's someone else in his dressing room, so he figures he counted wrong. Goes on to the next room and blunders into Lady Caroline in the raw. Poor jerk couldn't even see!"

Spraggue chuckled. "Did she send him scurrying or attack him?"

"You should have heard the screams! I thought one of last night's rats was chomping on her toes. Karen came down and smoothed everything out. Eddie's sharing his room with Gus, poor slob."

"Should we invite Gus in here?" Spraggue asked reluctantly. "It is bigger."

"No way. Let the lunatics stay together. He'd just take it as an insult, Spraggue."

"An insult?"

"Believe me. When he's like this, if you say hello to him, it's an insult." Greg paused for breath. "That beard makes you look older. I like it."

Spraggue changed the subject. "Time?"

"Four minutes to company call. Far as I can tell, Langford hasn't even shown up yet."

Spraggue grunted, concentrated on lining his forehead.

"And Emma *is* here, so it's not that. She didn't happen to come with you, did she?"

Spraggue glanced up. It *had* been Greg in that car last night. "No," he said evenly.

Footsteps echoed down the stone passageway, quick, loud, and angry. A door banged shut, swung open, and was firmly reclosed. Greg leaned out acrobatically into the hallway, turned back to Spraggue, and giggled.

"Judging," he said, eyebrows elevated, "by the *dramatic* entrance, the *majestic* footsteps, the *lateness* of the hour, I would say that the great Langford has arrived. And it sounds like he's throwing a fit of his own!"

Emma Healey, lovely in innocent Lucy's pale blue, hurried past the doorway.

"Ah, love," murmured Greg Hudson, "or should I say 'Ah,

144

lust'? Wonderful how these womenfolk do rush to their afflicted menfolk. No sooner had Grayling exited stage right in a huff, than little Georgina ran off to join him in his exile. Think I'll throw a tantrum and see who I get. . . . Deirdre's much too tall and grim. . . . Eddie, now, he's a dear, but so isolated, so lonely. And the stage manager's got a thing for him, don't you think? I don't suppose you'd come to my aid. I'm not particular. I'd take comfort from anyone, except, I think, Caroline. One has to draw the line somewhere."

The whistling started down the corridor—low, mournful notes, no familiar tune.

"*Who* is doing that?" Caroline demanded, voice shrill through her closed dressing-room door. "Stop it at once!"

"Bad luck." Hudson's face was grave. "Bad luck. Just what we need tonight."

"You believe that?"

"Well, I don't whistle in my dressing room and I don't quote the goddamned Scottish play. And I wish to hell somebody'd stop that *whistling*!" He raised his voice on the last phrase and hollered it down the hallway.

The whistling ceased.

Greg took a deep breath. "See? That episode upset Caroline. But does anyone go off to soothe Our Lady? Not our boy Eddie. He finds her a predatory old hag. Not you. Not me. Now, if our great director were here, or our rotund house manager, you'd see another story entirely. *They* care. If this weren't Arthur's play, that woman wouldn't be *near* a starring role. You can see it, can't you? She's not that good. She lets them all take it away from her—Langford, Emma—hell, she just about *asks* you politely to please steal the damn scene—"

Karen Snow's clear voice interrupted Hudson's outburst. "Green room in two minutes, please! Two minutes!"

Plenty of time. Dracula didn't make his entrance until the middle of Act One. Langford could dress after the meeting. Spraggue zipped his striped medico trousers and pulled on his jacket as he strode down the hall.

Despite their paint and powder, the actors looked unnaturally pale. Deirdre's lips moved silently; she had trouble remembering lines. Georgina and Gus Grayling stood off to one side, whispering united against the world. Hudson looked even paler than he had in the dressing room. Last night's drinking bout, or a more recent affliction? He was none too steady on his feet.

Darien arrived, to the actors' polite applause. Caroline, entrance neatly timed to follow the director's, came in and kissed Darien warmly. She squeezed his hand while he spoke.

Standard director's speech number two: thank you for your hard labor; give your all tonight.

Spraggue hardly listened. He kept his eye on his fellow actors. Emma Healey came in late. John Langford never showed.

The gathering was brief. Spraggue hurried back to his dressing room, knotted his tie, and powdered off his makeup.

The performance elapsed with all the sequenceless urgency of a nightmare. Scenes shot by, punctuated by applause. Lights dimmed, blackened, sparkled, dimmed again.

"It's not going too badly." Standing in the wings, Spraggue felt Karen's presence before he heard her whisper and only then realized how keyed up he was, every nerve primed for some new disaster.

"Did you notice the blooper Langford pulled?" she went on. "Must have skipped six deathless pages. Emma brought him right back, spoon-fed him the lines, while Caroline looked on with great cow eyes."

"Wish I'd seen it," Spraggue said.

"They'll razz him forever. The infallible British actor!"

Blackout. Karen disappeared. Spraggue flexed the tense muscles in his shoulders, took three deep breaths, walked onstage.

The curtain rose in darkness. Spraggue froze in his final scene position, stage right. Lights flared, glowing like a galaxy of sudden stars.

Greg Hudson spoke first, darting angrily around the set, searching the rocky crypt for the casket of the Vampire King.

HARKER: The Slovaks brought the coffin in here! I swear they did!

VAN HELSING: No exit.

HARKER: We'll catch them! Make them talk!

SEWARD: No time, Harker. The sun's almost down.

VAN HELSING: Come, if the coffin was brought *in* here, it must *be* here. Perhaps a secret panel? A hidden room?

SEWARD: A trapdoor?

HARKER: Take that wall, Doctor. I'll try this one. Professor, tap on the floor. Mina, help me.

VAN HELSING: She's weak, Jonathan. I doubt she can aid us.

SEWARD: Stay with her then, Professor. Jon and I will search.

Search they did. Forty-five seconds of busy silence with all the classic elements: life-and-death conflict, good colliding with evil, and a time limit—urgency. Spraggue and Hudson pounded the set, stirring up clouds of dust, listening frantically, intensely, for a hollow sound. They strained to lift papier-mâché rocks, felt in crannies for secret levers.

HARKER: How can we get in?
SEWARD: There must be a way—something—to—

Caroline laughed, a low, cunning growl.

VAN HELSING: She knows.
HARKER: Mina.
SEWARD: Help us, Mina.
MINA: You poor petty fools! You think you can defeat him? Here, in his own land?
SEWARD: Jon, take the pick. We'll break the wall down!
MINA: Fools!
HARKER: I felt something give! Keep working! The crack's widening!

With a snarl, Caroline threw herself on Hudson, tearing the pick from his hands. The fight was on.

All Hudson's careful choreography paid off. Caroline fought like a madwoman, shrieking abuse at the three men, determined to protect her Vampire Lord. Seward twisted the weapon from her grasp. Van Helsing caught her arms, pinned them behind her. The men carried her, kicking and screaming, downstage, away from Dracula's hidden lair.

Even the slap worked. Caroline turned with it, just at the crucial second. Great sound, no pain. She opened her eyes wide for one instant, sank to the ground sobbing.

HARKER: Mina! Darling!
SEWARD: She'll be all right.
VAN HELSING: Quickly!
SEWARD: The stake!
HARKER: No time! The sun! The sun!

Feverishly, the three men broke down the jagged wall, exposing the secret cavern. Stage center—a platform. On it, raked so that the audience could see the ornate carving, the elaborate scrollwork—the coffin.

Spraggue and Hudson sprang on top of the dais, shifted the lid off the coffin, staggering with its supposed weight. The Vampire King lay exposed to the audience, majestic, forbidding. Spraggue noticed beads of sweat on Langford's brow and upper lip.

The Vampire King opened his eyes.

VAN HELSING: Don't look at him!

Hudson's knife flashed in the spotlight. Spraggue drew his, pressed its blunt edge against Langford's neck. The chicken-blood pouch was in place; a crimson ribbon soaked through Langford's starched white collar.

Greg brandished his blade, grasping it in both hands. With a cry, he plunged it down into the Vampire King's chest. Blood welled up from the wound. Langford's scream changed to a moan, bubbled in his throat, and stopped abruptly. A gout of dark blood gushed from a corner of his slack mouth.

The actors froze. Spraggue's eyes met Hudson's, his hand reached for the stained knife.

The curtain fell.

Pandemonium!

Chapter Twenty-four

"Dammit, Spraggue!" Hurley shouted, pacing the corridor outside the dressing rooms. "Do you realize what you've done?"

Spraggue counted the cracks in the old stone floor.

"You were *worried* about something. Right, Spraggue? Nervous enough to get *me* here, anxious enough to have me lay free passes on off-duty cops! If I'd known we were being invited to a murder—"

"At least you're first on the scene," Spraggue interrupted flatly.

"And headquarters'll sure wonder what the hell I was doing here, all dressed up and sitting on my fanny, while some guy gets knifed!"

"Look, I read it wrong, Hurley. I never dreamed there'd be a murder. I still can't believe—"

"Believe it!" Hurley snapped. "Langford's meat."

"No accident? The knife didn't jam?"

Hurley lifted the weapon, carefully sheathed in plastic, from his inside breast pocket. "It's been printed and photographed. How's it look to you?"

"Normal. Except for the blood."

"Heft it. What about the weight?"

"I only handled it once or twice," Spraggue said slowly. Why did the knife seem so familiar?

"Try the mechanism. Carefully."

Spraggue pressed the knife tip against the wall. It didn't give. He pushed harder.

"It's not a collapsible knife," Hurley said. "Not anymore."

Suddenly the memory clicked. Brass daggers, crosses etched into their handles. . . . "Send someone up to the director's office, Hurley. Crossed over the mantelpiece. Two knives."

Hurley hollered upstairs, told a pair of heavy black boots to check Darien's second-floor room.

"You think the fake knife was modeled after the knives in the office?"

"Must have been. I should have realized—"

"Wouldn't a thing like this"—Hurley indicated the knife—"be checked before every performance?"

"It is. Send a guy to wherever you've stashed the crew. Have him yell 'Props!' A woman will answer. She's the one who checks the knife."

Hurley relayed instructions.

Spraggue dug his hands deep into his pockets.

"You okay, Spraggue?"

"No. If—*if* I'd thought someone was in danger, it wouldn't have been Langford."

"Who, then?"

"Darien."

"No use kicking yourself," Hurley said grimly.

"Yeah, you'll do it for me."

"Lieutenant?" Two pairs of black boots were ready to report.

"Foley?"

"One of the daggers over the mantel is gone. I took the other one over to Prints."

"Okay. Smithson?"

The other pair of boots hesitated.

"Smithson?" Hurley repeated.

"She's not here. The props lady. Death in the family. Took a plane out this afternoon."

"Who would have taken her place, Spraggue?"

Karen.

He was saved from answering by a commotion upstairs. Several deep voices barked orders, a soprano defied them. Doors banged. Spraggue stifled a smile. Aunt Mary. He pitied any cop who got in her way.

"Uh, Lieutenant Hurley?" Black-boots peered down the stairwell. "Problem up here. Lady wants to talk to you."

"About the case?"

Aunt Mary, pink and out of breath, pushed her way through to the bannister. "Certainly," she said with asperity. "Now tell these men to let me in!" She caught sight of her nephew and beamed. "I found him, Michael!"

"Whoa. Slow down there, Mrs. Hillman." Hurley took Mary's arm and guided her down the stairs, keeping her well away from Spraggue's warning glances. He propelled her into one of the empty dressing rooms and sat her down on a stool.

"I don't think my aunt knows what hap—"

"That's enough, Spraggue. Mrs. Hillman, you just told your nephew that you found him?"

"That's right, Lieutenant. I did. Just as you suspected, Michael. I came right over as soon as I—"

"*Who* did you find?"

"Arthur Levinson, Lieutenant. Associate professor of theater arts, Southern Methodist University. Have you ever tried to find a professor during summer break?"

"Does this have anything to do with—"

"It has to do with identifying résumé photos," Spraggue said shortly.

"Oh. Go on, Mrs. Hillman."

"Michael?"

Spraggue shrugged. "Tell the man what he wants to know."

"One of the actors is a ringer. Like with racehorses. He's using a legitimate actor's résumé and name, but he's really someone else. I have a picture of the real actor with me. Professor Levinson had it."

Hurley's foot beat a tattoo on the floor. "And the name of that actor is?"

Spraggue answered with her. "Eddie Lafferty."

Hurley turned on him. "You knew?"

"Knew, hell. Guessed."

"How?"

"The résumé he gave Darien was incomplete. According to his agent, Eddie Lafferty's done some major roles, even a *Hamlet*."

"Why not tell me about it sooner?"

"Tell you what? That our Eddie Lafferty doesn't look like my idea of Hamlet?" Spraggue rubbed a hand across his forehead, smearing greasepaint. "I didn't say anything, Hurley, because the kid's got blue eyes. The phantom I saw had dark eyes. And we had this trip-wire business—Eddie *prevented* a disaster—"

"A typical maneuver to throw suspicion elsewhere."

"That's what it looks like now."

"Foley! Smithson!" Hurley shouted. Heavy boots rushed down the stairs. "Where'd you put the actors?"

"You told us to stick 'em in that green room. Head of the corridor. Henry's with them."

"Let's go visiting."

"Let me come along," Spraggue said.

Hurley shrugged. "Suit yourself."

"Michael," Aunt Mary whispered. "What's going on?"

"Go home. I'll call you as soon as I can."

"We're going *now*," the detective said.

Spraggue followed Hurley down the hall.

The actors in the green room bore little resemblance to the tense, eager pre-performance crowd. Caroline Ambrose, her heavily powdered face ravaged by tear tracks, sat in a corner twisting her hands, toying with Mina's plain gold wedding band. Greg Hudson stood near the sink, an untouched cup of coffee in his hands, eyes fixed straight ahead. Emma, head bowed, sat on the sofa, an unmoving statue. Dracula's widowed brides hovered over her. Gus Grayling glared at nothing, his massive bulk in profile to the door. A tic in his lower jaw pulsed erratically.

"Edward Lafferty," Hurley barked.

The actors shifted, stared blankly around the room. Emma lifted her head, let it sink back.

"Spraggue?" Hurley turned to him expectantly.

"Where's Eddie?" Spraggue said calmly. He kept his voice low, all inflection deadened.

Georgina cleared her throat, tried her voice out tentatively. "He's not here."

Hurley rounded on the guard, the unsuspecting Patrolman Henry. "Why the hell didn't you—"

"Lieutenant, they told me this was everybody, everybody who was supposed to be—"

"And you believed—"

"Lieutenant!" Georgina's voice was firmer now, stronger. "It wasn't the officer's fault. Everything's been so confused—I guess we thought he might be in with the crew, with Karen—"

"Smithson!" Hurley bellowed.

"No, sir. No actors in with the crew."

Hurley grunted, turned to Spraggue. "You know the address?"

"Yeah."

"Good. I'll take two men and check it out. Want to come?"

Spraggue hesitated. "No."

"Okay."

He followed Hurley out of the green room, wrote Eddie's address on a scrap of paper, thrust it at the lieutenant.

"Sure you don't want to tag along?" Hurley asked curiously.

"I want to get this crap off my face." Spraggue tugged at his beard irritably.

"Suit yourself." Hurley spun on his heel.

"One thing," Spraggue said.

"Yeah?"

"Did your boys find a note? Near Langford's body?"

"Suicides leave notes, Spraggue. Not homicide victims."

"Right."

Spraggue waited until Hurley climbed the steps, his two minions struggling to keep up. Waited until their footsteps passed overhead, faded off down the corridor. If the actors were in the green room, where would they put the crew? Not backstage—too cramped, too crowded. Too easy for someone to stray. He mounted the stairs and knocked on the paint-room door. A red-faced, elderly cop cracked it open half an inch.

"Lieutenant Hurley wants to see the stage manager," Spraggue said.

"Ain't here."

"Not—oh." Spraggue was shaken.

"Try downstairs, first room on your left. They stuck her in with the actors."

"Thanks," Spraggue said through dry lips. In with the actors. Sure.

He bluffed his way past the guard at the double doors. The stage area was ablaze with light—each instrument focused on the raised dais in the secret cavern. All focused on Langford's corpse. Cameras clicked. A few officers shouted orders; some crawled on hands and knees, clutching plastic evidence bags.

Spraggue craned his neck skyward, searched the catwalk overhead. If she were still in the theater, where would the stage manager hide? He stared out into the auditorium, scanned the empty rows. The tiny, darkened lighting booth at the rear of the house almost blended into the back wall.

Spraggue approached the booth purposefully, a technician on his way to work. The door was closed, not locked. He entered, shut the door, reached for the light switch.

A hand closed on his wrist. "If you turn the light on, they'll be able to see us," said Karen Snow.

"Let them," Spraggue said roughly. "You've got nothing to hide. Right?"

"Spraggue—" she protested.

153

"Are you alone?"

"Yes."

"So you were dancing with Eddie when the lights went out last night—"

"I—"

"And because I believed you, Langford is dead."

"That had nothing to do with John—"

"You set me up." Sprague's eyes adjusted slowly to the dark. He pushed Karen back into the lone chair, kept his hands pressed against her shoulders even after she stopped squirming. "That night you 'helped' me with my blocking, Eddie broke in so you'd have an alibi—"

"I didn't know anything about it!"

"And then you arranged that farce at his apartment so I'd rule him out. You must have called Eddie just after I left the theater. A shame to let him stand on that chair too long."

"Eddie didn't kill anyone."

"Do you know who your Eddie is?"

"He's not *my* Eddie," she said sadly. "I just inherited him."

"And what is that supposed to mean?"

"He's my stepbrother."

Sprague placed a hand under her chin and gently tilted her face until their eyes met. "Then he's not your lover." He said the words softly, bit them off when he realized they were audible.

"What?"

"It doesn't matter," he said. Not anymore. And then aloud: "So you know his real name."

"Was I supposed to turn him in for changing his name?" Karen asked furiously. "He can act. He got the job through an audition."

"Which job? Company assassin?" Sprague straightened up, massaged the back of his neck with one hand. "I thought he'd go for Darien," he said almost to himself.

Karen reached for his arm, squeezed it tightly. "He had no reason to hurt John."

"But reason enough to hurt Darien," Sprague said. "Alison Arnold."

Karen looked away. "You know about her."

"Was she his sister?"

"Yes." Karen clasped her hands in her lap, stared down at them. "His *real* sister. His only sister. Maybe ten years older. . . . God, he idolized her."

"What's his name?"

"Gene. Eugene Arnold."

Spraggue drew in his breath. "You didn't say anything, didn't warn anyone?"

"What could I say?"

"And *you* didn't have anything against Darien?" Spraggue wished the light were better, wished he could see every line and shadow on her face.

"I never knew Alison. I'm not sure what happened seven years ago. Darien's one of the best directors I've worked for. He may have been an alcoholic. He's cured now."

"But you went along with Eddie's scheme."

"At first, I didn't know about any scheme, and then I couldn't stop him. Gene didn't intend to *hurt* anyone—"

"John Langford is *dead,* Karen."

"I watched Gene every minute he was offstage tonight. I told him I wouldn't let him interfere with a performance. I swear he never went near that prop table. Never."

Spraggue sat on the floor next to Karen's chair, cross-legged on the cold concrete. "Why did he run then?"

"He didn't run," she said firmly. "Give me the phone."

"Huh?"

"There's a phone on the counter, a few feet to your right. Dial 9 first. Now 555-6843. Gene'll answer. He just went home. I don't know why, but he just went home!"

Spraggue dialed. He held the receiver in his left hand, slightly away from his ear, so Karen could hear. Her dark hair brushed his cheek. The phone rang, seven times, eight, ten. Someone picked up the receiver. Karen breathed her relief. The voice was harsh, but familiar.

"Hurley speaking."

"This is Spraggue. Have you got him?"

"Nah. He's gone. Cleared out."

Karen's strong hands grabbed the phone, slammed it down in the cradle. The gesture seemed to drain her completely. "God, Michael, what am I going to do?"

He turned away, tried to forget the wildflower hair and soft brown eyes. What he wanted to do was hardly appropriate for time or place. "You have three choices," he said finally.

"Yes?"

"When the police question you, clam up, lie, or tell the truth."

"Any recommendations?"

"It depends—did Eddie set that trip wire?"

"No." She said it quick and strong. If she was lying, Spraggue decided, she was damn good.

"Then tell the truth. Believe me, the safest place for Eddie is in jail."

Chapter Twenty-five

Tell the truth. Shit. Four hours later, Spraggue jammed his clenched fists into his jacket pockets and strode down Massachusetts Avenue, too angry to stop and call a cab.

Of all the cops, they had to send out Menlo! Why not leave Hurley in charge? Hurley was a goddamned lieutenant! He'd worked Homicide! He'd been there, at the scene! Why Captain Hank Menlo, with his ugly, jutting boxer's mug and his negative IQ? The only time Menlo smartened up was in front of a TV Instacam. A publicity windbag, Spraggue had called him once, to his face.

Spraggue and Menlo were oil and water. When Spraggue had turned in his private investigator's license, Menlo had sent a congratulatory note.

"Poking your nose in again, I see." That was Menlo's idea of hello. The longer Menlo spoke, the more Spraggue felt his resolve to tell all weaken.

He'd tried. But he'd only gotten up to the part about Georgina's past when Menlo interrupted.

"And you kept that to yourself?" the beefy captain had shouted.

Spraggue hadn't bothered to answer.

"And here I thought you'd learned about obstructing justice when you were a P.I. Have to refresh your memory, I guess."

"How?" Spraggue had asked quietly.

"A few nights in the clink—"

Spraggue hadn't really meant to laugh, but he was pleased with the relaxed sound of the laughter. "I think you're the one with the short memory, Captain. Forgotten that last time you met up with my lawyer?"

157

"Then you had that damned private-eye card to hide behind—"

"Right. And this time I'm just a concerned citizen, helping out my fellowman. Please. Arrest me. Maybe with one more illegal bust on your record, you'll get tossed out for good. Do a hell of a lot for the image of the Boston Police."

Menlo had smiled, but his fingers had started tapping the desk just the way they used to. "Sergeant," he yelled. "Make me out a warrant. Georgina Phelps, alias Gina Phillips. Then get her in here. And tell the press—no, better yet, bring 'em all in here. I'll set up a conference—"

"Arresting her just to make the early-edition deadline, Captain?"

"Shut up."

"She'll be out of jail so fast—"

"Yeah? She got a hotshot lawyer, too?"

"You bet she does."

Menlo had raised his huge head, issued the snort that served him as a laugh. "Hurry up with that warrant, Sergeant. Have to be in time for the morning edition."

After that, Spraggue had answered yes and no.

He yawned; his jaw ached from clenching his teeth. He drew his hands out of his pockets and flexed his bloodless fingers, slowed his pace. Breathe in for four, hold for eight, breathe out for eight. His mind started to clear and he recognized his anger for what it was, fury at his own inadequacy. If he'd figured things right, Langford wouldn't have died.

He walked along Commonwealth Avenue, heading into Kenmore Square. Even that most frenetic part of the city stood empty at four A.M., the disco joints silent, the neon lights dimmed. Spraggue hailed a lone taxi, gave the Brookline address, and sat back to think.

"Mind driving with the dome light on for a while?" he asked abruptly, five minutes later.

"Nah. Maybe it'll keep me awake."

Even before he heard the cabbie's answer, Spraggue had his small notebook spread out on his knee, open to the page where he'd listed the joker's pranks.

1. Frank's Bloody Marys
2. Spraggue's decapitated bat
3. Georgie and Deirdre's decapitated dolls

4. Greg's bloody mask
5. Darien's dead raven
6. Caroline's dressing-room break-in
7. Eddie's attempted strangulation
8. Emma's bloodbath
9. Caroline's trip wire
10. Caroline's stolen orchids
11. Caroline's murdered dog
12. Alison's tape and the rats in Grayling's dressing room

At the bottom, he added Langford's death, number 13. Then, using the edge of his wallet as a crude ruler, he lined off a column to the right of the list.

Two tracks . . . that was the problem. Two totally different sets of footprints marched through the Dracula affair, twisting, intertwining, stepping over and under each other.

Eddie Lafferty was Eugene Arnold. *If* Karen was telling the truth, Eddie had meant only to frighten Darien, only to remind him of Alison Arnold's "accidental" death. Guilt and fear, those were Eddie's weapons. And he'd chosen *Macbeth,* Alison's final show, as the source of his messages to Darien. . . .

Which pranks had been accompanied by quotations? Spraggue ticked them off with checkmarks.

The beheaded dolls, the mask, the bloodbath. . . . Those had all come with act, scene, and line from *Macbeth.* Tricks played on the brides of Dracula, on Jonathan Harker, on Lucy Westenra. . . . He recalled that late-night conversation with Karen during his private rehearsal. Maybe Eddie *had* intended to follow the script, to attack Dracula's victims in order. . . . What about the other pranks?

No one had mentioned any message that went along with Frank Hodges's bloody drinks. That bat at the Fayerweather Street house, no message there. Damn. The printing. The printing was the same. . . . Spraggue temporarily shelved the objection. Printing was easy to imitate.

He ran his finger down the column. Six pranks accompanied by messages from *Macbeth.* Seven pranks unaccompanied by messages, including Langford's murder.

He rewrote the list, grouping the pranks, altering their order. The effort was hurried and his hand was jarred by the Beacon Street potholes and the cabbie's erratic lane switches. The result was barely legible.

159

A.	**B.**
1. The beheaded dolls	1. The Bloody Marys
2. The bloody mask	2. The beheaded bat
3. The dead raven	3. Caroline's dressing-room
4. Eddie's strangulation	break-in
5. Emma's bloodbath	4. Caroline's trip wire
6. Alison's tape, the rats	5. Caroline's stolen orchids
	6. Caroline's murdered dog
	7. Langford's death

Messages. . . . No messages.

But that wasn't the major difference. The pranks in the first column were scary, even gruesome. *But not one of them had caused any actual harm.* The second column was more malevolent. Frank had quit. Caroline could have broken her neck. Langford was dead.

Bits and pieces of conversation flooded back into Spraggue's memory: "Watch out for Langford; either he'll get himself appointed your deputy or he'll take over altogether! He's our chief busybody." ". . . psychological insights . . ." "Of course, that could have nothing to do with the joker." "I was afraid you might be too late."

While he had followed Eddie's trail, Langford must have tried to trace the other footsteps.

Just as the cab screeched into the driveway of the Brookline estate, Spraggue scribbled across the bottom of the page: A = Eddie, B = X.

Who the hell was X?

Chapter Twenty-six

Lights blazed on the first floor of the red-brick mansion. Never too late for Aunt Mary. She met him at the door, hugging a purple velvet dressing gown around her frail body.

"I meant to call," Spraggue said.

"I heard it on the news." She led him into the library, slippers padding on the polished floor of the foyer. "Do you want food?"

Spraggue shook his head.

"Coffee?"

"Please."

She poured from a silver pot. The fragrant steam bathed his face. He sat down heavily on the green velvet sofa, leaned his head back against an embroidered cushion.

"The whole thing makes absolutely no sense to me," Mary said angrily. "Why should that boy kill John Langford to get back at Arthur Darien? Why not kill Darien?"

"Exactly," murmured Spraggue. Aunt Mary stared at him expectantly, but he said no more. Finally, she yawned.

"I've been waiting for Georgina, poor child. Are the police still grilling her?"

"She's in jail."

"That sweet child? That tiny little—"

"No strength required for this murder. A child could have switched the real knife with the trick one—"

"But shouldn't that blond fellow, Hudson, have noticed? Shouldn't it have felt different?"

"I couldn't tell one from the other. But, believe me, the police are very interested in Gregory Hudson, slighted lover of Emma Healey, wielder of the fatal knife."

"About Georgina. Did you—"

"I called Max Shaefer. He's not sure he can get her sprung tonight. He'll do his best."

"He'd better."

Spraggue inhaled coffee. "Has Karen Snow called?"

"No. No calls."

"I gave her Shaefer's number, too, but I doubt even Menlo would toss her in jail."

"Menlo? *Our* Captain Menlo? Is he giving you trouble, Michael?"

"He can't take my license away, can he?"

"True. Did you find out why Karen Snow lied?" She waited but Spraggue didn't answer. "Are you awake, dear?" she asked after a while.

"Barely. Look, let me brood alone for a bit." He saw his aunt's disappointed face. "Thanks for the coffee. Thanks for everything. It's just—"

"I know. I'll go up to bed now." She leaned down and rested her smooth cheek against his unshaven one. "I'm sure you did whatever you could, Michael. . . ." Something in his eyes warned her to stop there. She turned and left the room, closing the heavy oak-paneled doors without a sound.

He must have been asleep when the phone rang. He burrowed into a sofa pillow and tried to recapture his dream. Puzzle pieces, there were puzzle pieces in the dream . . . tiny fragments that persisted in changing color and shape, even as he held them, grasped them with all his strength.

He opened his eyes reluctantly. The phone.

Hurley.

"Look, Spraggue"—his voice was muffled, urgent—"I just monitored a call from a District 4 patrol car. An attempted break-in at the theater."

"Attempted?"

"Amateur. Panicked when he heard the prowl car. The regular boys figure it was a kid, souvenir-hunting after the murder."

"And you?"

"I just figure it's interesting."

"You sending a man out, Hurley?"

"Haven't got anybody. Short shift. I can probably get somebody on it at seven."

Spraggue checked his watch: five-fifteen. He couldn't have slept more than fifteen minutes. "I'll go, Hurley," he said.

"You kidding? Menlo would have my head on a pike if he knew I was talking to you!"

"Is there a guard at the theater?"

"Nope. Menlo sealed it up tight and commandeered all the keys."

"Thanks."

"Wait a minute. What are you planning?"

"Try to see that nobody gets there until seven, okay?"

"You know how much say I have over Menlo—"

"Has he got Eddie yet?"

"No. But he's got an all-points out on him."

"How's it worded?"

"Armed and dangerous. You know Menlo. Shoot first, talk later."

"Hurley, see that the kid doesn't get killed. Tone it down."

"I'll try to tag along when they take him—"

"Thanks." Sprague hung up and stared at the phone. Five-eighteen. Leave the house by five-thirty. Half an hour to the theater. Maybe twenty minutes.

What he wanted was a long, hot soak, a shave, a change of clothes, orange juice, bacon and eggs. He slapped cold water on his face, shoved a note to Mary under the jade bowl, and left the house.

Chapter Twenty-seven

With a quick glance in the rearview mirror, Spraggue pulled to the left, into the narrow alley beside the theater. The right wheels bounced up on the curb, tilting the car at a rakish angle. Spraggue held his breath, but the Volvo cleared the tall buildings on either side by a good two inches. No scrapes, no scratches.

The alley sloped downhill, opened into a tiny trash-filled yard. Spraggue killed the engine and coasted to a stop. Five forty-five. Record speed.

He got out and pushed the door shut without slamming it. A fine snoop's car, Aunt Mary's Volvo; its deep blue exterior melted inconspicuously into a dumpster. Spraggue retraced his path up the alley.

The predawn chill was more like October than August. Spraggue wished he'd tossed a jacket over his black turtleneck. His left foot stepped on a shard of broken glass. He halted in front of the sheltered side door.

An amateur job, all right. The small window next to the door had been clumsily smashed. No glass cutter, no neatly shaped knob of putty, just rock versus glass. The hole wasn't large enough to admit a midget's hand. And whoever had made the hole had taken to his heels at the approach of a prowl car, giving the game away. If he'd stayed put, stayed quiet, the police would never have known.

Spraggue worked at the door with his picklocks, his face pressed close enough to hear the tumblers click. Once he thought he heard footsteps, but it could have been his imagination, or his heartbeat.

The handle turned. With a faint creak, the door opened. The small foyer was vaultlike, cold, damp, and still. Spraggue closed the door behind him, focused the beam of his tiny pencil flash on the floor. Karen kept flashlights on the pegboard in the wood shop. The wood shop was downstairs.

He padded lightly over the uneven floor toward the stairs. The damp chill rasped his breathing. He passed the costume shop, the storage rooms, the paint room.

Downstairs. Right turn. The trapdoor lift loomed in front of him, left open in last night's confusion. He'd come too far. He turned back, fumbling with his hands along the right-hand wall, until he located the pegboard, found a more suitable flashlight.

The new beam was clear and strong. Spraggue muttered a quick prayer for the contined good health of its batteries and set out for the stairs.

One hour. He'd have to be gone before seven, before the police arrived. One hour to search the cavernous theater, the offices, the dressing rooms, the storage closets, the work-rooms. . . . Might as well have stayed home.

One hour. Just have to trust to intuition, instinct, and luck. Something might work. Something *was* there.

What? Something that hadn't been in the theater when all the cast members had left at four, but was mysteriously there by five-fifteen? Mail sure as hell didn't come that early. No. Something that had been in the theater at four, but was too unusual, too incriminating to be removed under the eyes of the cops? Or something that didn't have to be removed, that had to be altered, changed. . . .

Spraggue decided to take care of his own business first, personal business. Maybe his intuition would be working by the time that was finished.

He jogged down the narrow hallway, turned right, and took the next flight up to Darien's office.

The door was locked, but the next office down, probably Spider's, had a communicating door that stood ajar. Spraggue shielded the flashlight, kept the beam low. The lone window in Darien's office was filthy and blocked by a mess of fake greenery; still, just as well not to risk a curious onlooker.

Darien's office was empty, still as a cat waiting to pounce. The faint outline of the missing daggers stood out against the far wall. Darien would have told the police when he'd last seen the two daggers, whose idea the trick replica had been.

Spraggue reached deep in the pocket of his jeans, pulled out thin plastic gloves, carefully smoothed them over his fingers. Then he followed his flashlight beam straight to Darien's single filing cabinet. He riffled the contents; all he wanted was one thing. There: Karen Snow, 2412 Westland Avenue, 555-7687.

He toyed with the idea of calling her now, waking her. Hell, what would that accomplish? Make sure she was home, find out what Menlo had pried loose. Later. He had fifty minutes left for the search. Damned effective search you could pull off in fifty minutes.

He played the flashlight around the room. Nothing. Papers. If Darien, or anyone else, had wanted a file, a slip of paper, that badly, he'd only have had to slide it between the leaves of a magazine, or into a roomy pocket. No need for a clumsy burglary attempt. If the burglar's target was one of the offices, why use the side entrance at all? The employees' door was closer, almost as well-hidden from the street.

Okay, intuition, time to get going. The side door . . . closest to the dressing rooms. Personal belongings would be stored in the dressing rooms. No valuables, of course. The assistant stage manager collected rings, watches, and wallets before each show. No locks on the doors. Too many anonymous individuals hurrying to and fro.

Langford's dressing room would be the first stop. Spragrue moved as he decided. If Langford had been killed because he'd caught on to X, he might have made some notes on his investigation, left some clue as to his "psychological insights."

Langford's room had been searched, a careful, polite, nondestructive police search. The evidence remained: heavy curtains pulled slightly away from windows, drawers barely ajar, carpet rolled up, crookedly replaced. The leading man's clothes were all jammed together at the end of the single rod; Langford had been a fastidious dresser. Spragrue's hands searched each jacket pocket, patted and probed. Nothing.

If the police had checked out the victim's dressing room, Spragrue doubted they'd neglect the suspect's. He entered Eddie's room and noted, with a sinking sensation, the same subtle signs of disarray. Still, he searched. Why the hell not? What could a well-trained group of cops find that Hawkshaw Spragrue couldn't? He quickly emptied all drawers, fondled their undersides. Nothing.

Eddie's makeup kit lay on the counter. Spragrue checked each jar and bottle, praying for something, anything out of the ordinary. Tubes numbered and labeled Max Factor and Jack Stein, tiny tins of color, crêpe hair, spirit gum, contact-lens solution—

Contact lenses. That's how Eddie had pulled off the dark-eyed, caped apparition at the theater. That's why he'd seen the trip wire. Spraggue grunted, cursed. Height, weight, eye color: the first questions the cops always asked, the first things the trained observer looked for. You can shave a mustache, but you can't change your eye color. Sure. So much for the old maxims of the trade. If he hadn't trusted his own eyes so much, maybe. . . .

Six thirty-five. Langford's room and Eddie's had taken too long, yielded nothing. A cop at seven, Hurley had said. Time to leave. He focused the flash beam reluctantly on the door.

Damn. Suddenly he knew, *knew* where the clue would be. Intuition, late, but still cooking. Caroline's dressing room. Too much had happened in Caroline's room: orchids stolen, room ripped apart, dog killed. Karen had sworn Eddie had never touched that mutt. Spraggue believed her; he'd seen the boy's face.

He pushed open the door to Caroline's room. No signs of search here. But then the police weren't working with the old Spraggue intuition.

The flashlight picked out the broad shelf running along the right-hand wall, the radiator, the vast expanse of mirror, the makeup-stained sink. Costumes hung neatly along a rod at the end of the room, headless corpses in the gloom. Caroline's last-act dress lay crumpled on the floor; her oversized makeup case on the shelf. Aside from some smeared tissues, it cast no reproach on its owner. Each item was neatly placed, closed, wiped clean of painted fingerprints. Spraggue removed a large jar of pale face powder, opened it, sniffed. His nose wrinkled at the smell—flowery, overripe, decayed.

He studied Caroline's photographs, ran his hands behind the frames. Caroline Ambrose receiving the Tony Award . . . with various stars, gushingly inscribed . . . with Darien, arms entwined, he minus the silver in his hair. Spraggue hesitated over a small image of a younger Caroline, embraced by a dark, mustached Latin. De Renza, that would be, the Colombian former husband. . . .

Nothing. He could find nothing in the room. Five minutes to seven. Nothing! Spraggue closed his eyes, leaned back against the shelf.

What was he looking for? Something different, something unusual. He pressed his gloved fingers hard against his temples. Two days ago, three days ago, he'd been in that very dressing room. Was anything different now? He played it as an acting exercise. Start with yourself: what had he been wearing? Yes. He felt the nubby tweed of the jacket against his wrists, the smooth cotton of the cream-colored shirt. What sounds had he heard? Faint hammering from the wood shop. Yes. Caroline in blue, a silky royal-blue dress, belted, and precariously high heels. Smells: her cloying perfume and—

Spraggue opened startled eyes, flashed his beam of light into all the corners of the room, clicked it off. Faint sunlight trickled through the one high slit of a window. The orchids were gone.

Orchids in a vase. Orchids in Caroline's hair. Orchids stolen. Orchids delivered daily. Spraggue touched his bare knuckles to the inside of the vase. Dry. No box, either. No square white florist's box lying under the counter. . . .

But he'd seen a box, seen it just moments ago, a sudden shape in a cone of light. Where? Langford's room? Eddie's? The office? No. The room next to Darien's office, the one with the connecting door. There, on the desk—

A sudden noise overhead shattered Spraggue's reflections. Footsteps thumped across the ceiling. Too late.

"Looks okay," came a distant voice, "but check it out real careful. I don't like that car parked back there."

"Right, Captain."

Spraggue didn't need the rank to recognize the voice: Menlo. More steps. They went up, to the second-floor offices. Flat feet marched in the corridor: Menlo, patrolling the only path from the basement to the main floor.

Just get from a basement dressing room to a second-floor office and then out of the building without being spotted. Sure thing, Spraggue. While you're at it, walk on water.

Spraggue traced the plan of the theater in his mind. One staircase from basement to first floor. Another staircase, twenty feet away down a straight corridor, from the first floor to the second. No other way up.

Menlo couldn't stay all day, wouldn't waste a man on stakeout. He could hide until the police were satisfied, wait them out.

He looked around. Not in Caroline's dressing room. Menlo's boots plodded overhead. Quickly, smoothly, Spraggue crept down the corridor, holding his breath as he passed the staircase. Destination: the wood shop. Full of machinery, piles of lumber, roomy closets: a far better locale for a game of hide-and-seek.

He recognized the trapdoor lift, passed it on the right, without thinking. Then he stood absolutely still, a faint smile twisting the corners of his mouth.

The lift was completely silent; it had to be. Several times no music covered its ascent during the show. The lift could get him up to the main level. After that? Who could say?

He abandoned the borrowed flashlight on a workbench. It was light enough now to do without. How did the lift operate? Surely not from the distant lighting booth; communication would be too difficult. Not from backstage. The elevator platform was bare of switches or levers. That would be too simple. But there, eight feet to the left, clamped to the wall: a power box. Yes. Dracula would assume his position on the platform. A stagehand would hit the button, propel the vampire magically upward.

Could he do it alone? Press the button, jump onto the platform, taking care to leave no dangling limbs behind. *If* the main power switch was on. He got ready—right hand back, extended toward the button, knees flexed, prepared to run.

The platform responded faster than he'd imagined. No start-up drone, no gathering speed. It took off. By the time he threw himself aboard, it was shoulder-height.

Thank God the wooden platform was uneven. He got a good grip on a raised board, swung his right foot up. The ceiling came closer, the open square allotted to the lift a mere postage stamp. Spraggue's left leg inched upward. His knee found solid ground. As the lift joined the stage floor, Spraggue lay thankfully huddled center stage.

With no windows, no lights, the stage was darker than sin. Spraggue cursed softly, regretted the lost flashlight. Intuition and instinct. Instinct had better get ready to take charge.

The staircase was temptingly close, just outside the double doors, but it might as well have been on some South Sea Island while Menlo's boots beat drum messages on the floor.

Was there a direct route between the stage and the second-floor offices? The stage house went up three floors, catwalk at the top. Too high. The side boxes; those were about the right height. The theater plans flashed back into Spraggue's head. The stage-left box. If there was any doorway, any window, it would be there.

A steel spiral staircase, little better than a fireman's pole, was the only path to the box. Spraggue groped his way up the narrow flight on hands and knees, tiny pencil flash clenched between his teeth.

The box was hung with heavy velvet curtains, a six-by-twelve room perched over the stage. The back wall should be the closest point to the offices, even a common wall. But was there a way through?

The velvet hangings were loose tapestries, covering bare walls. Choking with dust, Spraggue investigated beneath them, patting the walls with his hands in the impenetrable dark.

The voices were so muffled, Spraggue wasn't sure they were real. But as he straightened up and moved to the right-hand corner of the box, they got clearer, louder, until he could make out sentences, distinguish tones.

"Nothing up here." Menlo's assistant.

"We'll check out the basement." The captain himself.

Just over his head, Spraggue could see a faint grillwork of light. No doors, no windows, just an innocent heating vent. Maybe three feet by two. Big enough, once the cops went below.

Holding his breath, he waited for the sound of the slamming door and the footsteps on the stairs, then reached up and began prodding the screen. One corner was loose. He pulled it back, leaving a five-inch open triangle. He'd need more room than that.

With a stepladder, full light, pliers, and a screwdriver, the job might have taken three minutes. Working in the dark, half-smothered by velvet curtains, arms stretched uncomfortably over his head, fumbling at the screw heads with a dime, Spraggue lost all sense of time. One screw dropped to the floor, muffled by carpeting. Two. Three. Another loose one gave way with no effort. Sweat dripped down his face. He wiped his hands on his pants. One more. Then he'd bend the screen back, find out exactly what was on the other side.

Done! Spraggue listened carefully, then thrust his hands through the opening. The wall was maybe six inches thick. His fingers could grab the other side. He pulled himself up, spreading his elbows to take his weight, resting on the sill.

It was an office, one he hadn't seen before, empty except for a few sticks of furniture. He took a deep breath, hoisted himself up and through the narrow opening. Halfway, he rolled over, painfully. The vent was close enough to the ceiling to allow him a grip on the molding. Surprisingly, it took his weight. His hand found a water pipe, perfectly located. He chinned up on it. His legs scraped through the hole and he dropped silently to the floor.

This office, like the others, had connecting doors. He wouldn't have to risk the corridor. He went through another deserted office, then found the one he wanted. He froze, listening. Footsteps, yes, but far away. The police were still in the basement. He was almost afraid to look around. What if that momentary image of a white florist's box had been just that, an image only, a memory suggested by a square of white paper on a desk?

The box was there. Spraggue scooped it up, tucked it under his arm. Police in the basement; then this was his chance. He walked out of the office, took the steps in a reckless dive, and was out the employees' entrance before he'd really weighed the risks of an escape.

Once outside, the path was clear. 2412 Westland Avenue. With a jaunty step, he headed toward Karen Snow's apartment.

Chapter Twenty-eight

Karen's place was exactly what he'd expected from the address, one of the crummier student apartments huddled near Symphony Hall. Dirty gold brick with seven crumbling concrete steps up to a front door complete with cracked glass panes. He pressed the doorbell under the printed card: K. SNOW. The buzzer went off almost immediately.

He hadn't expected her to answer the door with such an expectant grin. But as she stared at him, the smile died on her pale face.

"Not all dressed up for me, are you?" he said ruefully, pushing past her unresisting body.

"I'm not—" she stammered. "You can't—"

"Come in here? I'm already in."

"Michael." She steadied herself on the doorjamb. "Please leave."

"Nope. Now that we've bypassed the formalities. . . . You're waiting for Eddie, right?"

"Gene," she corrected faintly. "I told him I was alone. I promised not to tell anyone—"

"Nice place," Spraggue said. He took a few steps down the hall, turned left into the living room, set the white box down carefully on the coffee table. One of its legs—about an inch shorter than the other three—rested on an ashtray.

"Furnished and cheap," Karen said, following him into the room. "Hot and cold running roaches. Will you leave?"

He studied the string wrapped around the white box. "Do you have a sharp knife?"

"Not sharp enough," she said through clenched teeth.

"I don't even think that's funny." He took out a pocketknife, selected a blade. "Do you have any eggs?"

173

"Yes."

"Then I'll make you breakfast after I open this. Scrambled with cream cheese and fresh chives. Orange juice."

"If there're any chives in my refrigerator, they're growing out of moldy oranges."

"Rain check. Butter?"

"Margarine. Maybe."

Spraggue wrinkled his nose.

"What's in the box?" Karen sighed and sat in a faded wing chair.

"You've given up on tossing me out? What's in the box is trivial, just life or death."

"Looks like one of Lady Caroline's."

"It is."

Karen giggled, raised a quick hand to her mouth. "And you're going to violate it?"

"You sound pleased."

"I can't remember the last time I laughed. The cops kept me until almost four."

"You must have been one of the last. Did it sound like they were making progress?"

Karen ran a hand through her hair. "How should I know?"

"What did they ask?"

"Questions under two general headings: knives and gossip."

"Well, you *were* the one assigned to check that knife. Did you?"

Karen's voice took on the drone of schoolgirl recitation. "When I heard that the prop mistress wouldn't be in, I glanced at the table to make sure everything was there; I didn't have time to go through and work every prop—make sure the damned fans opened and the—"

"What time was the table ready?"

"Six. And before that the props were in a locked case backstage. And," she continued before Spraggue had time to frame the next question, "the knife in the case was definitely the trick knife. Some stagehand tried it out while setting up."

Spraggue frowned. "So the switch was pulled after six. Langford didn't even get back to the theater until after seven—"

"Whoa!" Karen interrupted him quickly. "I saw Langford at a quarter to six. First one there after dinner. Bright and cheerful. Smiled at me and told me how nice I looked. I practically fell on the floor. I remember thinking how great it was that even an old-timer like John could get so high about a preview."

"Karen, at seven o'clock Langford came down to his dressing room, in his street clothes, no makeup. He slammed doors, cut the director's pep talk—"

"His performance was off," said Karen thoughtfully.

"So," said Spraggue, "what upset Langford between five forty-five and seven? Do the police know?"

"If they do, they didn't share the information."

"Maybe Eddie knows. Gene. He's on his way here?"

"He's got nobody to turn to. I thought he might call—"

"And he did?"

"Yeah."

Spraggue leaned over, took her hand. "There's no place he can hide, Karen."

She nodded briefly.

"Now I want you to watch me open this box. Closely. So if any police officer should ask you about it—"

She rubbed her eyes, folded one leg under her, and sank back into the chair. "Okay."

"You know how the orchids get to the theater, Karen?"

"Some messenger service. I think they're flown in from Colombia to Florida, from Florida to Logan. On De Renza's own planes, no less. A delivery company picks them up at the airport and whisks them off to Our Lady. What the whole setup costs—"

"You'd think he'd send them from a local florist."

"Orchids are one of De Renza's well-publicized hobbies. You couldn't duplicate his flowers anywhere in this country."

"Shall we see what kind of blooms the lady is missing today?" The sides of the plain white box were taped to the bottom. Carefully, Spraggue slit the tape with his pocketknife and lifted the lid. Creamy white tissue overlaid the inner box. He shook it out and placed it to the side. A layer of clear cellophane was stretched taut over the flowers, a half-dozen delicate white blooms with blushing violet centers. They lay on a bed of crimson tissue, held in place by long pins camouflaged in background greenery.

"If you slit the cellophane, Caroline will have a fit."

"Good idea." Using the knife, Spraggue neatly removed the thin plastic from the edges of the box and added the square to the pile of tissue.

"Do they smell?" Karen asked.

"Hardly."

She got up, leaned over the box, inhaled deeply, and sneezed.

"Bless you," Spraggue said automatically, a corner of his mouth twitching with a repressed grin.

"It tickled!"

Spraggue rummaged in his pocket. A tiny magnifying lens appeared. He examined the flowers, peered closely at the red tissue backing, the greenery. He removed the pins, then the orchids, one by one. He lifted the tissue.

"Here's what made you sneeze," he said. "In the bottom of the box. Just a few grains of powder."

"Why take it apart so completely?"

Spraggue moistened his finger, dabbed it around the edges of the box, licked it. "The rest must actually be *in* the box. Stuffed in those little corrugated ridges."

"What are you talking about?"

"What's Colombia's major export crop, Karen? Coke."

Her eyes widened. "Cocaine? In the orchids?"

"We just found the secret backer. An absolutely regular supply. Christ, De Renza's like a saint over there. Nobody would question his private plane—"

"Then he and Caroline . . . ?"

"I don't know. Could be him, could be someone who works for him," Spraggue said.

"Caroline never unpacks the flowers herself, Michael."

"Yeah."

"Did you expect to find drugs?" Karen had to strain to hear Spraggue's muffled response.

"Hurley warned me. When I first took this job, he said to watch out for cocaine. . . ."

"Hurley?"

Spraggue looked up, realized that he'd been thinking aloud. "Lieutenant Hurley. A good cop. If he plays his cards right, he'll make captain over this uproar."

"Michael, how much is there?"

"In this box? Probably not more than a couple of ounces. But if it's pure, you can double that. Cut it with milk sugar. Street coke's never more than fifty-percent pure. Twenty-eight grams to the ounce. Maybe $100 a gram. Fresh shipments coming in every day—"

"In other words," Karen said bluntly, "a hell of a motive for murder—"

The soft knock on the front door interrupted her. Karen's hand jumped to her mouth. "Michael, he's so scared. If he sees you, he'll run."

"He's doing okay. He must have waited until somebody else came in. No buzzer. At least he's still thinking."

"Go into the kitchen, Michael."

Spraggue grabbed her by the arm, spoke softly in her ear. "Remember, Karen, there's no place else he'd be safe. Don't get any ideas about slipping him five hundred dollars for a quick flight to Mexico. The cops are watching the airport, watching the bus stations. They could be watching this place."

"But I didn't tell them anything about Gene. The cop who questioned me was such a—"

"Menlo?" She nodded. "Say no more. But even if the police aren't on to him, the killer could be. I figured he'd turn up here. Everyone in the company knows you're close to Eddie. Answer the door."

"Michael? Can he get out of this? Do you see any way—"

"If he can help me nail Langford's killer, that should go over big with the cops."

"It'll be dangerous," she protested.

The knock came again, more urgent this time.

"For Christ's sake, Karen! Let him in! We've got a lot to do."

Chapter Twenty-nine

"For Christ's sake," Hurley echoed some eighteen hours later. "Stay the hell out of sight! If he's early—"

Spraggue plunked an aged and enormous Irish walking hat over his slicked-back hair. "Would you recognize me?"

Hurley curled his lip in disgust. "Where'd you find that suit?"

Spraggue tugged at a greasy lapel. "Want one for Christmas? I could probably arrange it since you've been so cooperative. . . ." He sneezed; the jacket was redolent of ancient cigar smoke and modern mothballs.

Hurley gazed at him severely. "Just be back in this van no later than one-thirty. Otherwise, I pack up the road show and wheel it back to headquarters."

Spraggue held out a wrinkled brown paper bag that cradled a $1.98 bottle of muscatel. "Last chance for a hit before I leave," he warned.

"Get out of here."

Spraggue extricated himself from the rear door of the van, taking care to slide unobtrusively into the shadows. His down-and-out drunk act didn't fit with the inconspicuous gray vehicle parked on one side of the Charles Street entrance to the Boston Public Garden. He was grateful for the crummy hat; it was just starting to rain.

He made a wayward circuit of the Garden, pausing often to hoist the muscatel. When, he wondered, had the neat signs describing each tree given way to clumsily gouged and intertwined initials signifying undying love? An occasional wino tipped his hat, but the drizzle served as a convenient shield. Man couldn't be expected to socialize with his head buried in his collar, shoulders hunched to ward off the chill raindrops.

All quiet along Charles, along Beacon Street, Arlington, Boylston. The glistening windows of the Ritz-Carlton dining room seemed worlds away, not just across the road. The rocking gait Spraggue had adopted for his skid-row character got more comfortable, felt more real. He traversed the central Garden paths, headed for the lagoon.

In the bright daytime, the lagoon was the bustling center of the Garden. Popcorn and ice-cream hawkers shared the bridge with the tourists, the field-tripping schoolchildren, the hurrying businessmen and women who craved the half-hour's sunshine more than their lunchtime tuna-on-rye. Clouds of colored balloons decorated the green bridge railings. Below, the graceful, elderly swan boats, bicycle-pedaled by vacationing Harvard students, steered precarious paths through V-shaped duck formations.

At 1:15 A.M. the bridge was empty. A semi-deflated pink balloon, string slip-knotted to an iron piling, hung forlornly down toward the dark water. An occasional courting couple strolled by, reflected in the glow of the high globular bridge lamps; the bums passed more frequently. Spraggue imitated their tottering steps as he descended the stairs on the Charles Street side, taking care to shield his face from the intrusive lights.

No one familiar in the Garden tonight. Not yet. The sudden noise of a cracking twig spun him around to face emptiness. His face relaxed into a grin. Less chance than usual of getting mugged in the Garden, with every other tramp a plainclothes cop. He wondered about that last entwined twosome crossing the bridge. Very romantic. If they weren't undercover cops, the police would probably find them breaking several statutes in the bushes by the lagoon.

The small tunnel under the bridge was the meeting place. Spraggue walked through casually, his eyes photographing the graffiti-blotched gray stone. An empty bottle of Southern Comfort adorned the path. For a moment the mist cleared, then he was back in the open again. He circled the lagoon once, dawdled by the Edward Everett Hale statue, headed back toward the van.

"Jesus," said the recruit who answered his discreet knock, "I was gonna tell ya the Salvation Army's up the road." He gave Spraggue a wide smile and a hand up. "You're soaked. Guys out there'll be bitchin' for days."

"Lieutenant up front?" Spraggue cut him off.

"Yeah."

One twenty-eight: Hurley was staring at his watch when Spraggue came in. One of eight walkie-talkies lined up on a narrow table suddenly crackled into life.

"Target One entering now from Boylston Street. On time."

"Any sign of—" Spraggue began.

"No," Hurley snapped. "Bad night for this. Drizzle makes it hard to see. Maybe nobody'll show."

"Maybe," Spraggue agreed. "Did any of them call the cops?"

"Just your Miss Ambrose. She came wailing in about dinnertime, going like a siren. We should have filmed the scene and sold it."

"Others?"

"Nope. We could draw a crowd—or a blank."

"Lieutenant?" The big tape deck, set up against the right-hand wall of the van, began to whirl. Eddie's whisper filled the van. "I'm going under the bridge now. Nobody in sight."

Hurley slammed his fists down on the table. "I told that kid not to contact me! I should have used a decoy!"

"A double could lure your murderer into the park, under the bridge, but he couldn't trap him," said Spraggue coolly. "I can see it in a courtroom. 'Naturally, I was curious, Your Honor. I wanted to know what could be in that box to make it worth fifty thousand dollars. I should have called in the police, I know, but—'"

"We'd have the money," Hurley said. "That's confession enough."

"*If* he brings any money. He might just bring his trusty knife. If at first you *do* succeed—"

Hurley wiped his big hands on his pants' legs. "I bet the kid'll blow it."

"I coached him. He's not a bad actor—should remember his lines—"

"He'd better."

"He's got a hell of a lot of motivation," Spraggue said quietly.

"Why doesn't somebody report in?"

"Stop stewing, Hurley! Think you'd never been on a stakeout before—"

"My ass is the one in a sling if anything goes wrong, Spraggue. You know what old Captain Menlo's like."

"Menlo's busy."

"Yeah. Working on a phoned-in hot tip. I'd just like to know if it was you phoned it in."

"He's out of the way, right? And if you cop Langford's murderer—"

"My life's going to be just peachy no matter how this plays out." Hurley looked so glum, Spraggue wanted to laugh.

Another walkie-talkie sputtered. "We got a guy entering from Arlington Street. Looks good. Nervous. Collar pulled up, hat pulled down—"

"A big, fat man?" Spraggue demanded.

"You know the talkies only go one way, Spraggue. You'll find out soon enough."

"How long do you figure it'll take him to get to Eddie?"

"*If* it's not some lonesome dude setting off for an evening's frolic in the Combat Zone—"

"Come on, Hurley!"

"Depends. He may be cautious, circle the park first. He may just decide to get the damn thing over with."

Sound came from the tape-deck speaker: someone clearing his throat. Spraggue concentrated on relaxing his neck and shoulder muscles. Time passed. Bells chimed out two o'clock. Something would have to happen soon or—

"I ought to turn you in to the cops." The voice over the speaker was low, whispery, but recognizable.

"Who the hell is it?" Hurley thundered.

Spraggue swallowed audibly.

"I brought you along on his little outing 'cause I can't tell the players without a program. *Who is it, Spraggue?*"

"Darien," he said.

"You thought it was the house manager, the one they call Spider, didn't you?" There was a shade of triumph in Hurley's deep voice.

"No," Spraggue answered flatly. "I knew it was Darien."

"Do that." Eddie's light tenor was surprisingly, tauntingly loud. "Call the police."

No noise. Darien hesitating? Maybe all the figures added up to a wrong conclusion. Damn tape recorders, anyway. Spraggue longed for a TV screen, a way to note the subtle shift in a forced smile, the sudden lift of an eyebrow.

"Why did you phone?" Darien asked.

"I told you. I have something that belongs to you. I'm not in a position to convert it to cash, so I thought you might like to buy it back."

"That's Caroline's, I believe." Good. Eddie must have shown

him the box. Spraggue nodded at Hurley. Everything according to schedule.

"I'm not asking you to buy flowers, Darien. You can buy silence, though—with a little nose-candy bonus."

"Five thousand was all I could get."

"That leaves forty-five to go."

"How will I get in touch with you?" Darien asked.

"You won't. I'll get in touch with you. On my terms. Believe me, you've got no choice."

A brief crackle.

"He's passing the envelope," Hurley said exultantly. "We've got him!"

"Don't go." It was Eddie's voice, unexpectedly harsh. "I'd like to count it."

"Hurry up."

"Don't order me around, Darien! I want to take my time, look at you, figure out what a woman like Alison saw in you—"

"Let go of me," Darien whispered.

Hurley's eyebrows shot up.

Eddie's voice was a grim monotone. "Listen to me, Darien. You're not getting away with it. Not because of Langford's death. Because of Alison's. Look at me. Can you see her in me? Can you? I've got you trapped, hooked and wiggling. This place is teeming with cops. I'm working with them. See this microphone? Everything you've said—"

A sound of ripping fabric, of splashing and cries, tore through the sound system.

"Jesus, Spraggue!" Hurley yelled. "You teach the kid those lines? Nice quiet arrest on the way back to the hotel—"

Hurley turned. He was talking to air. Spraggue had vanished.

The drizzle had intensified to bone-chilling rain. A gust of wind knocked Spraggue's hat to the ground as he ran toward the bridge. He couldn't see, but he heard the floundering in the lagoon, the squelching, running footsteps.

"Eddie!" he called.

"All right . . . I'm okay." The answering voice was weak, but close enough for Spraggue to get a fix on. He waded into the waist-deep lagoon, dragged out the sodden bundle.

"All right. Get Darien. Across the lake. . . ."

Spraggue entrusted Gene to two tramps who came running forward, suddenly alert. Then he splashed on across the lagoon, toward the far shore and a fast-fading, half-running figure.

"Darien," he shouted. The wind spat the word back in his face.

The silhouette disappeared, appeared, starkly outlined by a street lamp, then gone. Spraggue followed it. The lights at the park's perimeter were stronger. Flashing blue lights, swirling over police cruisers, marked the exits. Their beams herded Darien, drove him toward the center of the Garden. Spraggue's soaked pants' legs flapped about his ankles. He hoped Hurley had warned his men not to shoot.

Darien ran for the bridge, bent over, stumbling. Spraggue cursed; his left shoe, lagoon-soaked, tripped him up. He kicked it off.

Darien was halfway across the bridge when the cruiser parked on the other side flashed its brights. He turned back; Spraggue blocked his path. The director retreated sideways toward the railing, pressing his back against a stone column.

"Don't come any closer!" His voice was wrenched by great grasping breaths, but surprisingly strong.

Spraggue heard Hurley answer, voice mechanized by a bullhorn. "You're surrounded, Darien. We won't hurt you—"

Something glinted in Darien's right hand. "I have a knife," he said.

"There's nothing you can do with it," Hurley replied firmly. "Put it down."

"Spraggue?" Darien turned to face him, the glare shining off his reddened eyes. Spraggue felt the silent support of policemen at his back. Darien's gaze shifted. Spraggue knew that if he'd been alone, Darien would have tried to take him. Thirty years' difference in age, a foot in height. No matter. Darien's eyes were mad.

He surveyed the situation—water below and to his rear, police on either side. He measured the distance from bridge to water, a paltry eight-foot flop into muddy ignominy, no glorious Golden Gate dive. Through it all, those wide staring eyes never faltered; he kept the knife pointed, hovering in a wide semicircle. His mouth opened and closed and a harsh sobbing sound emerged. It took Spraggue a long time to realize it was laughter. When Darien finally spoke, his voice was totally controlled.

He talked to Spraggue as if they were alone—kind-uncle-anxious-to-explain. The knife circled; the eyes flashed warily from side to side. "I always wanted to do *Macbeth,*" he said, as if it were the natural beginning to a conversation on a bridge in the middle of the night, dead in the sights of five S&W six-shot revolvers. "Do you want to know why?"

From across the bridge, Hurley nodded eagerly. "Why?" Spraggue asked, too loudly.

"Because I find the ending so powerful. You remember, 'I will not kiss the ground before young Malcolm's feet.'"

"Yes," said Spraggue. "Throw the knife in the water, Arthur."

"Macbeth was wrong, wrong throughout the play. He traded honor for calumny, love for hatred." Here Darien's voice wavered. "But Macbeth dies a hero! That's how I would direct it. He knows he'll die, but still he fights. 'Lay on, Macduff/And damned be him that first cries, "Hold, enough!"'"

It should have been ridiculous. An old man with a knife, rain and tears pouring down his face, quoting Shakespeare to the police.

"Kill me," Darien pleaded. "I will not yield."

"No one's going to kill you," Hurley said. "Put down the knife."

"You still don't see. Don't you know what I was? I drank, Spraggue, but I was a great director. People should remember my name, not like Nichols, not like Papp, but like Stanislavsky, Meyerhold. The classic men of the theater—"

"Like Samuel Borgmann Phelps," Spraggue said.

"Yes. But the pressure, the *pressure*. I drank. And they knew. And the scripts stopped coming. No one would trust me; no one would back me. I needed that money, Spraggue. To prove myself again. It would have worked. This play would have put me back on top, where I belong. Don't you see?"

"But Langford got in the way?"

Darien tried to laugh, failed. "He knew. He came to me like some bright Boy Scout brimming with his news before the show. He never suspected I had anything—"

"Spider," Spraggue said.

"Yes. He thought Spider was pulling the strings. No one ordered me around, Spraggue. *I* ruled. What was Langford? An actor, a puppet. I made him dance; I won him applause, awards. Me. I could do that for any actor. For you. What did I need Langford for?"

"Put down the knife, Arthur."

"No." With his left hand he unbuttoned his coat, loosened his shirt.

"Macbeth would never kill himself," said Spraggue.

185

The director turned to him, a smile lighting up his mad eyes. "I remember. 'Why should I play the Roman fool and die on mine own sword?' Right? 'Whiles I see lives, the gashes do better upon them.'" As he spoke, his voice grew wilder, stronger. He hefted his knife and dove at Spraggue.

"I can handle him!" Spraggue cried. "Don't shoot!"

He jumped back, and the tip of the knife sliced by him, an inch from his chest. Blue light glittered off the blade. He ripped his sodden jacket off, wound it around his left forearm, used it as a shield, drawing Darien closer, waiting for Hurley to get in place, to twist the dagger from Darien's grip.

He reckoned without madness. Darien fought like an animal, writhed, slashed; a shrill stream of abuse escaped from his bubbling mouth. The knife caught Spraggue's shirt-sleeve; a thin line of fire burned down his right arm. He hooked a leg behind the director's knee, tripped him up, and pounced on the hand that held the knife.

The battle changed; Darien no longer tried for Spraggue. He twisted the knife in, toward his own face, toward his eyes. They arm-wrestled in grim sweaty silence.

Other hands reached to help. Blue-clad bodies knelt at Darien's side, surrounded him. The director cried out, went suddenly limp.

"His heart! How's his heart?" The voice must have been Hurley's.

"I don't know," Spraggue gasped.

How Darien pulled it off, how he twisted out of the melee armed with a police revolver, no one knew.

"Don't—" Spraggue cried. His words were drowned in the blast of a single shot. Darien's gun clattered to the ground. His hand reached up, grasped his side. He took a long time to fall.

Hurley bent over him, shaking his head as his fingers searched for a pulse.

"He didn't have a—" Spraggue began. He looked down at Darien's calm, baby-round face, white hair plastered down across his forehead. He shrugged, swallowed twice. "Christ, you did him a favor."

Spraggue stood on the bridge, leaning against a column, deaf to all questions. He unrolled his jacket, put it on slowly. Inspected the cut in his arm: a scratch. Then he pulled his collar up around his ears and walked away. Voices called after him. He kept walking. After a while, the drumming rain blocked out all other noise.

Chapter Thirty

"You sound terrific," Hurley said after Spraggue sneezed for the third time in two minutes. "Drink?"

Satch's, behind police headquarters on Stanhope Street, was almost empty at three in the afternoon. They slid onto two bar stools.

"Just coffee," said Spraggue. "Black. I'm all doped up on antibiotics."

Hurley gave his order to the barmaid. Bourbon on the rocks. Spraggue raised an eyebrow.

"Coffee," Hurley muttered sadly. "And here it was gonna be my treat. Serves you right for wandering around half the night soaking wet. I almost put out an APB—but I figured it might look bad: loony millionaire dressed up like a vagrant. What would people think? And with your luck, Menlo would have been the one to spot you. He'd shoot on sight."

"What's he want?" Spraggue asked, annoyed. "His case is solved."

"*My* case, Spraggue. I'm grabbing a lot of points on this one. I'll be out of Records so fast—"

The drinks arrived. Spraggue tried to smell his coffee, gave it up. The steam felt good anyhow. He cradled his cup. "So that explains the celebration."

"And I thought you might like to know that we picked up your friend, the Spider. Got him at the airport."

"Congratulations."

Hurley sipped bourbon. "You know, based on those calls your boy, Eddie, made, only one out of four citizens calls the police when threatened with blackmail. Caroline Ambrose was the only one who came to us. Darien—well, Darien had reason not to. Spider heads for Miami—"

"Probably bound for points South American."

"Right."

"What about Hudson?" Spraggue asked. "I was sure he had nothing to do with it, but he threw me with that total failure to react."

"Says he just figured it as one more prank. And he's real busy consoling that redheaded wonder woman. I'll bet she put it out of his mind."

Spraggue drank hot coffee.

"I bear greetings, too," continued Hurley. "Your little blond friend is out of jail. She sends her undying thanks. If you'll call her, she'll say 'em in person."

"Yeah."

"The other one, Karen Snow, asked me to give you this." Hurley thrust a small square envelope into Spraggue's hand. "She left town this morning, with her stepbrother. Going up to Maine to see the family. No one pressed charges."

Spraggue turned the slender envelope over in his hands. Just as well, he thought. If she hadn't fooled him so completely—

"Don't you want to know what Spider said?"

"Sure."

"Spider really started the whole business—" Hurley began.

"By blackmailing Darien over that car accident?"

"You got it. Darien was dead drunk. Spider saw it all, from the backseat of the car, no less. By judicious use of shady connections, he got Darien off the hook—for future considerations. Darien *had* a real future back then, before he got labeled a drunk."

"When did the cocaine come in?"

"While visiting friend Caroline down in Colombia. Spider was bleeding Darien pretty good by that time. Darien got inspired, smuggled a little dope back to the States, just enough to keep Spider off his back. Later, after Caroline left De Renza, Darien figured out a way to take advantage of the orchid scam."

"He had a confederate in Colombia?"

"One of De Renza's assistants. As far as De Renza knows, he only sent Caroline floral tributes for one year."

Spraggue smiled. "That'll be a blow to a king-sized ego. Think she knew what was going on?"

Hurley shrugged, tipped back a slug of bourbon. "I doubt she wanted to know. I'm sure she never questioned her popularity as a Darien leading lady. Only the critics did that."

"The one time she talked to me about her pals, Spider and

188

Darien, her dog died. Spider must have let her know there was a connection between the two events."

"Spider admitted killing the dog."

"And what else?"

"Oh, he was anxious to confess, to everything but murder. That honor he gives to Darien."

"Funny how all the pieces fit together," said Spraggue.

"Make me laugh, then. I still don't get it all."

"From the beginning?"

"Great place to start."

"Okay. Gene Arnold gets himself cast in Darien's play. He borrows another actor's résumé; the real Eddie Lafferty's probably off on some European tour. Gene's goal: to give Darien a severe case of guilt. Maybe even scare him out of the business.

"Darien panics. He wants protection, but he's afraid to go to the cops because of the cocaine. So he tries a couple tricks of his own."

"Get me another bourbon," Hurley said to the barmaid. "Which tricks?"

"He gets rid of Frank Hodges via the Bloody Marys. If that hadn't worked, he'd have tried something else. Because he wanted me to come in and catch his joker. And to hook me, he sent me the bat, imitating the joker's printing."

"So all the small stuff was Eddie's? The dolls and the—"

"Here. I've been through this." Spraggue pulled his black notebook out of his pocket, opened it to the page he'd scrawled in the cab. "Take a look."

A	B
1. The beheaded dolls	1. The Bloody Marys
2. The bloody mask	2. The beheaded bat
3. The dead raven	3. Caroline's dressing room break-in
4. Eddie's strangulation	4. Caroline's trip wire
5. Emma's bloodbath	5. Caroline's stolen orchids
6. Alison's tape, the rats	6. Caroline's murdered dog
	7. Langford's death

"A is for Eddie?" Hurley asked.

"Eddie or Gene, whichever you prefer."

"Your handwriting stinks. B for Darien?"

"Darien and Spider."

"Okay. So the first two pranks on the B list are designed to bring you in."

"Right."

"Stupid move."

"Darien's. Spider never approved of me."

"And the break-in to your leading lady's dressing room?"

"Spider, I think. He must have dropped one of the orchid boxes, spilled some coke. So he broke a jar or two of Caroline's powder as a cover-up."

Hurley's finger moved down the list. "Caroline's trip wire?"

"That threw me almost as much as it threw Eddie. Darien must have finally concluded that Caroline's performance could sink the show. He was in a bind. He *had* to use her; she was the cocaine source. Eddie's tricks gave Darien the idea. *If* the leading lady was injured, if she broke a leg, for instance, orchids could still have been sent to her hospital room. It would have been tricky, but I'll bet Spider could have found a way to arrange her flowers for her, and get ahold of the coke-filled boxes. Darien would get the money. He'd have Caroline in a local hospital, *and* he'd line up a great replacement."

"The stolen orchids?"

"John Langford. Pursuing his own detective inquiries. If he'd said anything to anyone else, he might still be alive. But he trotted his discovery straight to Arthur Darien."

"And Spider killed the dog," said Hurley.

"Yeah. And Darien killed Langford."

"Can I borrow the notebook?" Hurley shoved it into his back pocket at Spraggue's nod. "Sure you don't want a drink?"

"It wouldn't help."

"How about another puzzle piece?" Hurley tried to keep the satisfaction off his face.

"What?"

"The theater."

It took Spraggue a minute. "The Acme Holding Company," he said under his breath.

"Huh?"

"Aunt Mary tried to find out who owned the place. She ran up against some holding company."

Hurley nodded. "Darien. That's where all the cocaine money went."

"What'll happen to the theater?"

"Probably tear it down. It's a white elephant. Unless some rich young out-of-work actor decides to buy it—"

Spraggue finished his coffee, got to his feet.

"Let it rot," he said.

He walked out the door, Karen's envelope still unopened in his hand.